Wakefield Press

# The Noon Lady of Towitta

Patricia Sumerling is an Adelaide-based professional historian who believes some of the unresolved tales she comes across in her work are ripe for unravelling and for imaginative reconstruction as distinctively South Australian stories.

I0642781

By the same author

*Down at the Local*
*The Adelaide Park Lands*
*Elephants and Egotists*

# The Noon Lady
# of Towitta

Patricia Sumerling

**Wakefield
Press**

Wakefield Press
16 Rose Street
Mile End
South Australia 5031
wakefieldpress.com.au

First published 2010
Reprinted 2011, 2014, 2017

Cover designed by Mark Thomas
Edited by Julia Beaven
Typeset by Wakefield Press

National Library of Australia Cataloguing-in-Publication entry

Author:         Sumerling, Patricia, 1945– .
Title:          The noon lady of Towitta / Patricia Sumerling.
ISBN:           978 1 86254 941 8 (pbk.).
Subjects:       Schippan, Bertha – Fiction.
                Schippan, Maria Augusta. 1878–1919. – Fiction.
                Murder – South Australia – Towitta – Fiction.
                Trials (Murder) – South Australia – Towitta – Fiction.
Dewey Number:   A823.4

Wakefield Press thanks
Coriole Vineyards for
their continued support

*for*
*Roger Andre,*
*who made this novel possible*

# Prologue

## 2 January 1902

Detective Bill Priest was urgently recalled to duty on the second day of the new year as the city of Adelaide took refuge from the holiday heat. A telegram had arrived at police headquarters: a girl had been brutally murdered near Towitta, at the Schippan family farm.

'Where the hell is Towitta?' Priest asked Sergeant Decker.

'Well, the telegram came from Truro, so it must be somewhere round there. Sedan's near there too. The place is full of German families on farms.'

Priest and a large company of troopers prepared to travel to the murder scene and later that day boarded the train at North Adelaide for Freeling near the Barossa Valley. Extensive equipment and stores were needed for what could be many hot, windy days in the middle of nowhere. After settling the numerous horses, wagons and stores in the cattle trucks, they took their places in the passenger carriage set aside for them. On the journey north, Priest pondered the name Schippan. It was not a common name but he'd been involved with several cases where it had cropped up. He remembered a domestic servant named Mary Schippan whose friend had died after an illegal operation while working for a well-to-do city family a couple of years earlier. He had had trouble in convicting the well-known Adelaide abortionist responsible for several other botched cases. When he finally managed to obtain corroborative evidence he was able to have her locked away for several years. It had been difficult to find any woman who would tell on her, so popular were her services in Adelaide. He'd have been happy to see her hang for the several deaths she was responsible for. He recalled that she'd have been headed for the gallows but for an unfortunate technicality in the law that meant she got off with her life. He smiled as he pictured her behind bars.

The name Schippan also featured in a case near Sedan where a tyrannical German farmer named Mathes Schippan was involved in a shooting several years before but was acquitted by the courts in Adelaide. There were other disturbing allegations about him that couldn't be proven. One case was the murder of a hawker near Sedan. For some reason Schippan was not arrested although he was under suspicion. Priest soon learned that Mary, the servant involved in the abortion case, was Mathes Schippan's daughter. Considering this German farmer had been involved in several acts of violence, as was his daughter to some degree, Priest kept an open mind about what he might find at the farm. He kept his thoughts to himself about what he already knew of the Schippans while he became familiar with the intricacies of the Towitta murder.

Priest thought it ironic that in the first brief mention of the murder in the newspapers, the journos labelled it 'the Towitta Tragedy'. There was no tragedy about it as far as he was concerned. It was a brutal, savage killing, where the victim, a young girl, was butchered like an animal. Her throat had been repeatedly slashed from ear to ear and she was stabbed at least forty times in a frenzy by someone who knew how to use a knife. No, it was hardly a tragedy.

After many years on the job, Priest had come to learn that nothing was what it seemed and it made no sense to jump to conclusions. To do so would make it harder to find a new theory should the first one not stand up to scrutiny. Priest had been looking forward to a challenge such as this, for over the last few months he'd been involved in some pretty mundane cases. He had been following the sensation in South Africa where Australian soldiers were being tried for killing a Boer priest in cold blood.

The murder scene at Towitta was two days' travel by horse from Adelaide. Taking the train from Adelaide to Freeling and then travelling by horse through Angaston to Towitta cut the journey by half. On arrival at Towitta it was his responsibility to see that his band of troopers was sent around the district to find suitable places to board, while others camped in tents at the farm. It was also his task to organise the investigations and inquest. Priest planned the gathering of evidence and compiling of reports like a military operation. He had to ensure that no stone or speck of dust was left unturned in finding out what had taken place.

Priest and his men broke their journey overnight at the police station at Angaston.

'What's the gen?' Priest asked the two local constables on duty.

The older one, Constable Beckmann replied. 'Well, word is an unaccountable man was alleged to have broken into a farmhouse late at night and for no reason cut a girl's throat from ear to ear. It was surrounded by a lot of mystery and a great deal more running for assistance than running at the alleged intruder.'

'Really?'

'Yes, really, so the search is for some shadowy person who broke in, didn't steal anything and didn't even bring his own knife with him to do the horrible deed?'

Priest butted in, 'A straightforward case then?'

'If only. And to wrap it up nice and neat he left no footprints and was seen by nobody as he fled the area.'

Priest asked, 'What about the rest of the family?'

'As far as we have been informed the girl's elder sister, Mary, was able to struggle free with minor cuts and raise the alarm by running to the barn where her two brothers slept. They won't be much help, I believe they're rather simple. She then sent one of them to their closest neighbours for help. Apparently, there were two older brothers but they left home a couple of years ago after bashing up their father. Revenge, according to local gossip, for years of beatings and whippings.'

3

'Who on earth would have been wandering around in the middle of a hot night in the middle of nowhere?' Priest asked.

'Sir, the district is rife with gossip about the Schippan family. There is a lot being said about old man Schippan – he was a tricky character when crossed, I believe.'

Priest nodded. 'I remember a case six or so years ago when Schippan shot a youth. Hartwig, I think his name was, a real troublemaker. Old Schippan claimed he shot him accidentally.'

Constable Beckmann said, 'We also know now that the two sisters and their brothers were on their own. Their parents had left the farm two days after Christmas to spend time with relatives at Eden Valley. We've already had locals popping in here to try and find out more. There's lots of talk about the fact the two single young women were left on their own with two simple brothers.'

'I wonder whether any local man, such as a sweetheart, would have known that they were on their own?' asked Priest.

'It could well have been a stranger passing through, a hawker or commercial traveller up to no good. Although the chances of this seem unlikely, don't you think?' Constable Campbell replied.

The older constable coughed and waited until all eyes were on him before announcing: 'It seems that Mary Schippan has said that the intruder had an English-sounding voice when he threatened to kill her.'

'Hmmm, I can see we'll be having to do a door-to-door on this around the district, especially as there are so many opinions and gossip about the family.' Priest glanced at the darkening sky and his men making camp in the police yard. 'We have an early start. I'll go and join my men now.'

Priest and the mounted troopers rose before dawn the next morning and made their way through Angaston and down the treacherous Parrot Hill to the Murray Plains twenty-five miles away. He surveyed the plains from the top of the hill, drought ravaged and the colour of a desert. The sand drifts glinted red and released spirals of dust when the wind blew. This was Priest's first visit to the area for some time and he was alarmed at just how desperate the conditions really were. While he was thanking his lucky stars that he didn't live down there himself, he remembered the staff at the police station in Angaston telling him the Murray Flat farmers were better off than many others because they at least had the luxury of rabbits for food.

Priest pondered if that would make much difference. The little township of Towitta must have suffered a miserable existence due to the punishing drought conditions. It was no wonder that someone's nerve had given way in such a desolate place. Looking down the hill to the small scattered farms in that burning South Australian heat, he wondered how often it happened that a peaceful township became notorious overnight due to an act of murder.

Once at the tiny township of Towitta, Priest discovered that the population that used the scattered group of buildings, including a post office, a school, chapel and store, totalled seventy people living in just fifteen houses. The district was made up of many small farms covering around 200 acres each. Sedan, not quite seven miles away, was mostly settled by German families and Angaston was twenty-five miles away up steep and treacherous hill roads. Thirty years before, the Germans in the region had spilled over onto the plains from the more fertile valley of the Barossa, their heartland and spiritual centre.

The scrub country on the plains which extended eastward to the River Murray was usually favoured with fair annual rains, but not in the last year, Priest noted. He knew some farmers were quite well-to-do, but this did not include the Schippans or their neighbours. The nearby hilly district leading down onto the plains had miles of dry-stone walling, but as the red dusty soil drifted with the wind it banked up alongside and covered them. Towitta was a meeting place of the winds that swooped to earth here from all points of the compass and licked up as much dust as they could carry. After camping in the district for a week, Priest would learn that a gritty red sand mixed with an impalpable powdered limestone continuously floated across the plain, or was borne high in the air by a gust of wind before gently settling on all below.

Towitta was on no map that Priest had, and he doubted that any Australian soul would have heard of it when the reports of the murder hit the newsstands. Most of the residents in the region, including Schippan, had settled there after crown land was divided into small farm blocks. Schippan had lived in the area for over twenty-five years and, like everyone else on the plains, was struggling to survive the present gruelling drought. Located more than a mile away from tiny Towitta, the Schippan farm was in the middle of nowhere with barely a blade of grass, bush or tree to break up the dreary flat land-scape. Three miles away, on the western horizon, the Mount Lofty Ranges broke up the otherwise monotonous view.

When the mounted troops reached the farm, Constable Mowbray from Truro was standing by the gated entrance to the property. He was keeping all those with a ghoulish interest at bay, for already the news of the murder had spread far and wide. As they rode into the dusty farmyard Priest noticed two lads and a woman sitting in the shade on a long bench beside the thatched farmhouse. The woman sat staring ahead. Neatly dressed with a white pinafore, she had her hand on the head of one of the boys who lay with his head on her lap and was gently crying. The other, older boy looked sullen as he whittled pur-posefully at a mallee root with a large razor-sharp butcher's knife. They sat there waiting for who knows what.

Priest, in a horse and carriage, led the procession to the biggest barn. As they arrived the elder boy walked slowly over and asked, 'Sir, can I look after the horses?'

'I would be very much obliged, young man.'

The troopers climbed from carriages or sweating horses and headed for the water pump and troughs for a welcome drink and a cooling down. Priest noted that the smaller boy had dried his tears and had been summoned by his brother to help with the horses. Priest left the men and walked to the farmhouse where he was greeted by Constable Rumball and taken through the kitchen to an inner room.

'Prepare yourself, sir. What you're gonna see isn't very pretty. Though I'm sure it's better than what it was, for Lambert, the local constable, and his mum have put the corpse, Bertha Schippan, on the bed.'

Priest was quick to reply, 'Goodness, they shouldn't have done that before we arrived.'

'Oh, I dunno, sir, it was probably the best thing as it's been over thirty-six hours now, and it's pretty shocking in the bedroom. I mean we haven't touched the blood or anything but we've had to cover her over with a sheet. You'll see why.'

Priest was shown into the tiny bedroom where the body of the young girl was laid out under a sheet on a double bed. Now he could see why she was moved and covered. Swarms of flies buzzed noisily about the stains and splatters of black congealed blood on the floor where Bertha had lain. Priest knew the funeral was well overdue for the temperature hovered around a hundred degrees in the shade and the peculiar smell of death was already fouling the air. He grabbed his laundered neckerchief and covered his nose as he learned that the local coroner and doctor had already done their examinations.

The brothers, Wilhelm and August Schippan, who Priest was told did the heavy manual work around the farm for their father, helped him in any way they could. It didn't take long for Priest to notice that they were somewhat slow and sluggish. When asked questions it took time for them to reply, and indeed they appeared reluctant to do so, whether out of shyness or lack of English Priest couldn't say at first. The older boy was simply quiet, but his brother was strangely afflicted. As Priest spent more time with them he realised both brothers had problems speaking English.

The troopers soon discovered they had similar problems with the locals who were mostly first- and second-generation German migrants. While they, like the brothers, were most anxious to give the police all the help they sought, it seemed that the presence of a German linguist or a German-speaking police officer other than Deckert would have hastened their enquiries. As it was, they were greatly handicapped because of the lack of understanding of English by some of the locals. It was like being in a foreign country.

When Priest visited witnesses he couldn't fail to notice the excitement provoked by the shocking crime. It caused a thrill of horror in the minds of the honest hard-working German settlers. Such a thrill, he thought, would have been shared just as much by Adelaide folk who were as eager to hear the latest news of tragedies and homicides. Visiting the hotel bars in the district at Sedan, Cambrai and Truro over the following days, he heard the case enthusiastically debated, with theories advanced and refuted and the many suspects, whoever they were, already hanged in the imagination. Rumours of all kind circulated. No one had seen so many police in the district before. Priest noticed that the younger women gazed with wonder at the sight of so many young bronzed troopers going about their important duties.

Miss Mary Schippan was not one of the women who viewed the men in this manner. She appeared uninterested in them but she recognised Priest from the time, more than two years earlier, when her friend, a servant, had died at the hands of an abortionist in Adelaide. Mary appeared emotionless as he questioned her, looking past him as though in a trance. She moved little and her voice showed no trace of the suffering she must have felt after her terrible ordeal. Maybe she was in shock.

Priest sent the troopers to assist in a systematic scouring of the countryside. Every house within miles was visited. Every stranger was seen and interrogated and every clump of mallee examined, with no result. As he remarked to one of the journalists, 'If any man visited the Schippan house, as described by Miss Schippan, he has vanished completely into thin air as if he employed an airship to escape by.'

In the midst of the search, Mr and Mrs Schippan arrived home from Eden Valley. Priest went out to greet their buggy and tell them what had happened to their daughter.

'Goot afternoon,' Mrs Schippan said, her voice tightly controlled. 'Vee have driven here as fast as vee cout. Vee are very upset that something dreadful has happened to von of our daughters. Tell us please vhat has happened.'

Priest helped them down, their faces grave.

'I am very sorry, Mister and Missus Schippan, but your youngest girl, Bertha, has been savagely attacked and murdered by an intruder. We are doing all we can to find the perpetrator of this barbaric crime. What I can say is that your other three children are safe, although distressed, as you can imagine. Mary has suffered a few cuts and bruises.'

On hearing this, the shocked Mrs Schippan hurried to Mary. Priest took Mr Schippan to the house and led him into the bedroom where his dead daughter lay. Carefully he drew back the sheet and asked him to identify Bertha.

'This is Johanna, Mister Schippan?'

'Ya, but vee call her Berta,' he replied quietly, and reached for his neckerchief.

'Bertha, right. I'll cover her up now. The flies are pretty bad, I'm afraid.' They returned to the kitchen.

'Mr Schippan, we have seen what we need to and now that you have identified Bertha she must be buried as soon as possible.'

'Ya, I can see that, Mr Priest. There is an undertaker in Sedan.'

'I have some notepaper here. Write a note to him and one of my men will ride there for you. Inform him that he must come early tomorrow morning with a coffin. My trooper will also make sure the clergyman you need will be at the graveside in Sedan for a ceremony later in the day. I am sure you want relatives to know too. I'll leave you to write all the letters you wish delivered. There's pen and ink in my writing box on the table. Write the notes you need and I'll send some of my men off to deliver them.'

Mathes Schippan looked distraught and Detective Priest placed a comforting hand on his arm and said quietly, 'This is a terrible affair Mr Schippan but while I'm here my men and I will do all we can to lessen the burden you and your wife are suffering.' Applying a little extra pressure to Mathes Schippan's arm, Priest continued, 'Now, Mr Schippan, you can see how much mess this brutal murder has made to your home but we are still looking for clues. I'm afraid no one is allowed beyond the kitchen until we have finished our search. We can't afford to miss any traces of whoever was in the house with Mary and Bertha. After the notes are written I want you and your sons – with help from my men – to construct an outside kitchen with a cooking and eating area. It has to be large enough for your family and all of us. Then you need to re-arrange your barns for your family to sleep in for a few nights.'

Priest noticed that Schippan's sons were soon helping their father to carry out these instructions. But there was no chatter between them. Rather the boys appeared scared of their father, flinching when he came near. Mrs Schippan sat with Mary on the bench in the little shade there was, and Priest heard raised voices followed by the sobbing and weeping of Mrs Schippan. Mary never lost her composure. When Mrs Schippan finished her relentless questioning and it was quiet between them Mary continued to sit calmly, staring out across the paddocks. Frequent outbursts followed, Mrs Schippan working herself into hysteria and sobbing while Mary remained composed.

Mulligan the coroner and Steele the doctor compared notes and at four o'clock they gathered in the large implement barn for a coroner's meeting. Mr Mulligan sat at the head of a table that had been brought from the kitchen and asked each of the senior staff about what had been found. Although it was obvious from the moment they first saw the corpse that they were dealing with a murder, the meeting was held to confirm that death resulted from multiple stab wounds inflicted by what appeared to be someone in a frenzy. The evidence indicated several attempts at slashing the throat with a knife, similar to the one found in the kitchen – or was it that one? It took little effort for the police to find half a dozen bloodstained butchering knives around the farmhouse and in the barns. And it was likely there were others still to be found.

Within an hour the meeting was closed and plans were made to have the official inquest six days later in the same barn. Priest groaned at the thought of being holed up in Towitta for the next few days. But important procedures had to be carried out, such as the hunt for clues by the Aboriginal tracker. He hadn't arrived yet and who knew what he might find. Priest pinned most of his hopes on these clues.

It had been quiet, hot and still when they arrived at the Schippan farmhouse. By the next day conditions had deteriorated dramatically. The wind started in the night and with it the real hardships began. A high wind blew all day, carrying with it clouds of red gritty dust. There was no relief from the blinding choking curse that stung the face and made everyone miserable and snappy. Priest reckoned that the wind was strong enough to bury an idle person in half an hour and blow away a foot of Towitta every day. He resorted to covering his nose and mouth with his neckerchief. The place was not far from how he imagined hell to be. At least he knew he could return to Adelaide, unlike the poor local farmers. He had been told the farmers were sentenced by restrictive land regulations to reside on the plains nine months in the year, an unfair form of persecution he believed. It was a mockery that the native meaning of 'Towitta' was fresh water.

By the end of their second day in the district Priest felt he was coming to know the Schippan family. Even though he'd heard it said by many in the district that the family was held in the highest respect, looked upon as a model family and described as sober, industrious and affectionate, he wondered whether his leg was being pulled. There was plenty of evidence to think otherwise. He must face the question of what went on behind closed doors, as well as consider the acts of violence that Mathes Schippan had committed. Priest noticed that interactions between Mary, her brothers and Mrs Schippan appeared normal, almost affectionate. This was not the case when Mathes Schippan was involved. Any family dealings with him appeared difficult and strained. Although Priest never heard him raise his voice in anger, his family jumped to his commands. In fact, he never seemed to speak unless he was ordering someone. Priest began to wonder if Mathes Schippan had been involved in the murder, yet he had been more than twenty miles away when the murder took place, according to his testimony. But if Mathes Schippan hadn't done it, who else would do such a thing? And why was Mary not murdered instead – or as well as Bertha?

People were adamant that Mary was not a 'flighty' girl. Rather, she was known to have a nervous disposition and an obsessive fear of the dark that meant she was indoors well before nightfall. Priest observed that she may have been quite pretty once, but she was overly thin. This thinness and the way her hair was styled made her look deceptively tall. Like many spinsters with long wavy hair, she wore it pinned up on her head offset by a crimped fringe. The drab dark-brown of her clothes set off her deathly pale skin with its sprinkling of freckles over her nose and enhanced the reddish streaks through her pale-brown hair. Her face was strained and pinched and Priest never once saw her smile or relax. In many ways Mary was a younger version of her mother. Even the slightest smile would have changed her countenance. But then she had little to smile about.

It was said that when Mary and her older sister, Pauline, were young girls they created their own world of make-believe and acted out fairytales that reflected the reality of their lives. They dressed up in old clothes of their mother's or aunts'. Crowns and veils were made to turn them into princesses and queens, or the lovely daughters of a peasant or wicked parent. Their brothers, August and Wilhelm, roped in to be monsters, beasts, dwarfs or huntsmen, revelled in their odd roles. They were naturally ghoulish and loved any excuse to act out the brutal killings that were a part of many fairytales.

When not playing these roles, Priest was informed that the younger brothers loved killing whatever moved, whether birds or animals. They enjoyed dissecting the animals and generally scaring everyone with hoaxes and tricks that included animal blood and offal. He knew living in a dreary and isolated place such as this was partly responsible for the bizarre behaviour that several of the Schippans' neighbours had mentioned. Some folk in the nearby township were convinced the boys were the devil's work. But to be fair, it was probably because they were not the full quid.

Priest turned his attention to Mary Schippan and the possible motive of revenge. Did she have feelings of resentment against the actions of a girl not quite fourteen, an innocent girl? Or was she innocent? He'd already heard from an outspoken farm labourer that the young Bertha, a rising beauty and far prettier than her older sister, was rather precocious. Bertha did not share the family's fair complexion. Mathes Schippan told Priest, 'Berta inherited her striking dark looks vrom her long dead großvater, you know – and her gypsy character.'

Priest asked him to continue.

'Ov all my kinder, she vas the most difficult. Always spoilt rotten by Pauline, my oldest tochter, when she was alive. Don't know how she did it, but I can see she had me round her little vinger. My vife used to wring her hands in despair when Berta vas bedevilled because she knew I should lock her up or give her a touch of the whip, but I never did. I just couldn't.'

Priest considered whether Mary, ten years older, had been jealous of Bertha's youth? And Mary had a sweetheart. What had been going on there? Did her sweetheart, Gustave Nitschke, look in Bertha's direction and Mary found out? Priest had been told that Bertha had been forbidden from attending the New Year's Eve dance in Sedan. Had she set up a constant cajoling, perhaps threatening to tell her father of Mary's indecent behaviour with Gustave? If the inevitable punishment of a sound whipping by her father was simply too humiliating for Mary to contemplate, revenge could have been a possible motive. And the father's violent past provided reason for suspicion too, yet he was away in Eden Valley.

Priest could see that Mathes Schippan's control over his children was all but total. He treated his family as his property, preventing them from having lives of their own. The two eldest sons had run away from home, and the eldest daughter had died of tuberculosis. Being afflicted, the youngest brother was cursed to remain forever an ageing child. The youngest of the children, probably the smartest, had been brutally murdered. And then there was Mary, the tuberculosis she had suffered for several years sapping her energy, leaving her to accept her lot. Her one possibility for escape, if she was well enough, was Gustave Nitschke.

Priest knew it was crucial to get to the bottom of what had gone on between these two sisters between eight and eleven o'clock on the evening of the murder. They were referred to as 'loving sisters'. Surely Mary would not have resorted to murdering her sister?

The Schippans' house had been left unattended after the murder until the following morning when Constable Lambert and his mother and the three Schippan siblings returned. Mrs Ann Lambert then laid out the body before returning home. Certainly there was plenty of evidence of blood all about the house, over the floors and up the walls. With so much animal butchering going on around the farm it was hard to tell what blood was what.

On the Sunday after Priest and his company of men had arrived, Tommy King, the famous Aboriginal tracker from Gladstone, joined them. Originally from Alice Springs, he had earned an outstanding reputation on the trail. Accompanied by Corporal Finch he soon made a circuit of the Schippan house at the distance of about half a mile, but failed to find any trace of footprints other than those of the police and other visitors. Even with gales blowing throughout the day it was hard to baffle an expert tracker. Tommy told Priest with conviction, 'No fella come along there. No tracks here, Boss.' But Priest had a suspicion that even supposing foreign footprints had been made in the vicinity of the house, they would now have been blown away by the terrific dust storms. Perhaps Towitta itself had disappeared?

Priest told his troops, 'I don't care if all the dust storms of the Sahara have swirled to the Murray Flats, we will not abandon the enquiries, meaning none of you are going home until I am satisfied that all avenues have been pursued. Is that clear?'

Corporal Finch went with Tommy into the farmyard as he continued his meticulous search for tracks, but to no avail. There was no trace of bloodstains beyond the kitchen door and they were certain no one left the house at the time of the murder. The search by the troopers, a two-mile wide sweep, was extended beyond the farm. All that was found was the print of an old boot of Mr Schippan's in a dried-out puddle from long ago. The hopes that had relied on Tommy's skills blew away with the dust and left Priest frustrated and baffled.

The inquest had to consider these facts, of course. The evidence from inside the farmhouse directed suspicion to Mary. Priest was convinced that the father could not have committed the crime. His men rode from Eden Valley in daylight to see how long it took. They concluded that attempting it at night was simply not possible. One of the troopers volunteered to try but had to abandon the attempt. The evidence was pointing to Mary, and Priest was finding it hard to accept.

# 1

# Mary

*April 1919*

I have consumption. For eight years after my father's death I thought I was getting better because I felt free from his tyranny. How wrong I was. After Christmas, when I had several serious fits and bleeding bouts, Mother was so alarmed at the thought of losing me, her last remaining daughter, that she brought me for treatment at the Adelaide Consumptive Home. I'm told that once you come here you don't leave – except in a box. My prospects are hopeless.

Apart from its lovely but neglected gardens, the place has little cheer. According to the nurses, the hospital was once a lunatic asylum; that is perhaps why there are so many tiny cell-like cubicles with big iron locks on the doors. I have one of these old cells to call my own with a tiny window overlooking a shady garden. The rooms are in the long narrow building which everyone calls 'the corridor'. And it is here that other women patients like me will die.

Amid such gloomy surroundings, one of the nursing sisters almost half my age has befriended me. Although she's not from a German family like ours, Sister Kathleen tells me her family comes from the Barossa Valley, near where I have lived for most of my life. She understands my situation and we have become friends. She tells me of her sorrow for her sweetheart who was killed fighting near the end of the war in Europe. She bears this loss alongside the day-to-day squabbles between her, another nursing sister, seven nurses and the matron. The daily shenanigans provide us with much amusement; there isn't much else here to make us laugh. Without Sister Kathleen, I would have no idea of the 'goings on' in the hospital.

For my part, I tell her of the hardships of living on a farm for years dogged by drought, and something of Father's harsh treatment of my brothers and sisters and myself before they either died or ran away from home. I tell her that both my sisters died young, but I have not said how. It is touching that she is treating me as an equal. In the Barossa Valley and on the Murray Flats, where so many families of German descent settled, it is our lot to be treated as inferior or foreign because of our so-called peculiar customs and a foreign language and church. As for 'blocker' families like ours mixing, it simply wasn't done. Then, as now, it is always them and us – the British and the Germans.

We sit on the tiny verandah shaded from the warm sun with Sister Kathleen holding out her arms with my skeins of wool wrapped around her wrists as I wind balls. I pass much of my time knitting baby clothes for a church orphanage. When Sister Kathleen sweet-talks me into yarning about my life I find telling my own brand of tales still comes easy to me. We might spend just ten minutes together or as much as two hours, but these longer periods are rare as she is kept very busy.

After years of not saying much to anyone, I found it wasn't hard to tell tales in the way I once used to. So I began to look forward to her visits. I can't do much else now anyway, I have plenty of time to think of the tales I will tell her. Not long after we met she asked me straight out if I was that woman in the Towitta tragedy. She was plumping up my pillow at the time and asked, casually, 'Miss Schippan, I know you'll think I'm nosey and you can tell me to mind my own business if you wish, but Schippan is not a common name. I can remember our family talking about a murder in a family that had that name when I was a girl, and I'm sure there was a woman called Mary. Was that your family?'

I was caught off guard and hesitated. It may have been only

seconds before I replied, but my whole life flashed before me. I liked Sister Kathleen for she made a point of coming to see me whenever she was on duty, even when she wasn't rostered for duty to the 'corridor'. You couldn't ignore her because, despite the recent loss of her sweetheart in the war, she was bright and cheery. People like her make all the difference in a place where so many have low spirits, and she lifted mine without really trying. I made a hasty decision to answer her question honestly. What did I have to lose?

'Yes, it was my family. And if you don't mind me pointing it out to you, you're a brave one asking questions that don't really concern you, Sister. I hope you don't go about asking other women such personal questions. You'd be told you were nothing but a sticky beak. But I know that since arriving here a few weeks ago you've done your best to make me comfortable as well as make me laugh. So please, don't keep calling me Miss Schippan, just call me Mary.'

Sister Kathleen came round to the front of the day bed, grabbed my hands and looked straight into my eyes. She told me she had grown up knowing of the Towitta tragedy, as it was referred to in the newspapers of the day. Once we started to talk about this part of my life she enjoyed revealing to me what a thrill it was to talk to someone like myself, though I failed to see why. So yes, I admitted, I was notorious for being put inside a prison awaiting trial for murder. Prison was a world she knew nothing about and she was curious. She asked me if I was willing to share such memories. Well we will see how we go. I told her she would have to be patient with me as I needed time to think about what tales I would share.

I found that after keeping secrets for so long, being asked to talk of this time was like someone taking the stopper out of the bottle containing an impatient genie. And so we always spoke about my life and family, rarely hers I noticed. I let her rush on with her own views about the Schippans, because until now I'd never discussed them. The trouble was where to begin.

I thought the next time we met and if she had enough time, I would tell her about the life of a Wendish family in South Australia. It would take time to explain how one family came to suffer so much misery. I thought of keeping her interest by telling her a little at a time of our family, unfolding our story like a fairytale. This would give her a background to my life and how I ended up in this prison of a hospital. It would also help to make the days go by, though I know there are few left for me. But from the night following that first talk the nightmares returned.

## 2

My father had told me and my brothers and sisters the story of his life many times as we sat around the kitchen table in the evenings. What he didn't remember or chose not to tell, his sister, Aunt Giscelia, told us when we stayed with her. Like Father she was a good storyteller and made the family's trials and tribulations sound more like nightmarish fairytales. From these tales I thought I had learnt all there was to know about Father's and Aunt Giscelia's life in Germany, their journey to South Australia, and their life when they arrived.

But that night, after the first probe by Sister Kathleen, my peace of my mind was spoiled by having to think again about my family's past. I lay awake reliving the events that befell my parents, my brothers and sisters, my grandparents and myself, pondering on the life of my father. From the time we were old enough to listen he told me and my brothers and sisters chilling tales of his early life in the Fatherland, intending them as a warning. He told us they were true stories that we should believe and learn from. But fact was twisted with fiction making it difficult for us to tell what was real and what was make-believe.

When Sister Kathleen next visited I was impatient to tell her about my father's and his sister's early life in Germany. 'I know you said you wanted to hear my family's story but I don't know if you will believe me because it was so tragic. Are you sure you really want to hear all this?'

'Of course I do, Mary.'

'All right, but it is a long story and will take many days to tell.'

So I started to tell Sister Kathleen a story of events that happened long before I was born, so bizarre that it seemed not connected to me in any way.

Mathes – my father – and his sister were rescued from a bleak forestry life and adopted by their uncle and aunt when he was about ten. My grandmother and grandfather endured great hardship in their foresters' life. According to the family legend, my grandparents had met at the annual Cottbus May Day fete. After catching the roving eye of the gypsy-like musician, Josef, who was travelling with a group of troubadours, Mascha had run away with him when they moved to the next town. They travelled as entertainers until Mascha fell ill shortly before her first baby was due and they settled near his parents' homeland on the borders of Bohemia and Silesia. Josef became a forester and they lived in a hut on the edge of a dark medieval forest. They never found time for a wedding; snow, mud, rain and new babies seemed to delay all their good intentions. While my grandmother was in labour giving birth to Giscelia, her first-born son, barely able to walk, tottered off into the forest and was lost. Only after the dramas of the birth did they miss him. Weeks later when they found his remains they deduced he was killed by a wolf. This tragedy put the young couple on their guard and made the long black nights fearful and menacing for their two surviving children, my Aunt Giscelia and Mathes, my father. They were forever wary of marauding wolves, creatures of the night and other threatening shadows of the forest.

When Mathes was just six, his mother, Mascha, barely survived a difficult birth during which her baby died. The complications so soon after an earlier pregnancy maimed and crippled her and she never recovered. She was confined to bed and became weaker each day until her death six months later. After Grandmother Mascha's death, Grandfather Josef took to alcohol that made him wild and mad. He brewed almost pure spirit in the forest and sold some of it to those in the nearby village who knew of his still. But most of it he drank himself. Mascha and Josef had lovingly cared for and protected the young Mathes and Giscelia, but after Mascha's death the children were neglected.

One day, several years after their mother's death, their Aunt Katie-Lizzie and Uncle Herman paid an unexpected visit. News of Mascha had reached them from well-meaning family friends visiting the Zittau area in Upper Lusatia, centre of the Saxon linen trade. These family friends were passing through the district and had happened to stay at an inn in Zittau. Here dark and sinister tales about the nearby forest were told around dinner tables and winter firesides. Among these stories was the tragic but romanticised tale of the runaway girl from Cottbus who had lived on the edge of the forest with a wayward forester. After her death he went mad through grief, they said. Not only had the newborn infant died, but their eldest child was taken by a wolf. Although the event had taken place in the district four years earlier, the story was often spoken of as though it had only happened the day before.

Their friends' ears pricked up when they heard that the young girl from Cottbus was called Mascha. They guessed she could be their friend Herman Schippan's long-lost sister. My paternal grandmother's family had spent ten years trying to find her, never knowing she had already been dead four years when their friends stumbled across her family.

Herman was excited yet wracked with guilt when he heard that his cherished sister had left two small children to be brought up by a half-crazed father. Herman and Katie-Lizzie were about to migrate to South Australia with their only child, Gretel, but Herman knew he could not leave Germany with a clear conscience without first seeing what he could do for his sister's shattered family. They were kin after all. Herman and Katie-Lizzie immediately made the long journey from Cottbus to visit the family before their sea voyage to South Australia.

As they had never met Mascha's lover, they stayed at an inn when they arrived in Zittau. After finding out where Josef and his two children lived, Herman and Katie-Lizzie were driven by the innkeeper several miles out of town to the edge of a dark forbidding forest where there was a small hut in a clearing.

They intended to make themselves known to Josef and perhaps help him financially, but they were so alarmed at what they found that they decided that the best way of helping the family was to give them a chance in life by taking all three of them to South Australia with them, even if it meant delaying their voyage for some weeks.

Josef thought he had been saved from Hell when he met Mascha's family and welcomed them with open arms. Mathes and Giscelia, who were never seen apart, clutched hands and cowered together when their aunt and uncle first set eyes upon them. But when they heard their aunt's soft voice and her encircling arms pulled them to her ample warm bosom they felt soothed; the cold, the fear and the hunger disappeared. They began to cry, sobbing out all the woes of their short bleak lives.

Aunt Giscelia told her aunt and uncle that before her mother died she remembered her parents being happy despite their poverty. But after her mother's death, the agonies of bereavement exacerbated by having to support two motherless children made life unbearable for Josef. The three-roomed hut was mean, with nothing worth salvaging even for the children's sake except a children's storybook bound in green leather that he gave to Giscelia for safekeeping. Giscelia was still deeply affected by the loss of her mother. Mathes, quiet and sullen, had taken on Grandfather Josef's peculiar traits and habits. Come the night, they both became fearful and agitated.

In 1854, within a month of their blessed abduction, the new Schippan family migrated to South Australia from the port of Hamburg. Forgoing their original passage when they were to travel with their friends, Herman and Katie-Lizzie were able to secure a passage in the *John Moller* that plied the same route. And the green bound book of Grimms' fairytales went too, secure in Giscelia's care, all the children owned to remind them of their mother as they travelled to the far side of the earth.

Plucked from gloomy forests, bogs, snow, rain, howling

wind and the immense cold, they were taken to a land of heat, dust, flies, drought and barren landscapes. Nothing prepared them for such extreme change. But although the landscape may have been strange and new, their old fears, prejudices and strange Wendish customs and folklore travelled with them.

Despite the best efforts made for the new life Josef and his two remaining children were to begin in a new land, tragedy struck on the long sea voyage to Australia. Josef had become fatigued from seasickness as the *John Moller* battled the great Southern Ocean. Perhaps he clambered onto the heaving deck that was continually awash with mountainous waves to purge his stomach to the elements. Whatever happened that night, the wind screamed through the rigging as it had done for many days, with Josef probably hanging onto the leeward railings as he retched over the side without thought for his safety. It was only with the pale dawn, when the children were unable to find their father, that the alarm was raised. The ship was travelling at too great a speed through big seas to turnabout and no one was sure when he went missing. The ship's crew and passengers were saddened and alarmed. Some passengers tried to show extra sympathy to Josef's two small children but they clung more tightly to Aunt Katie-Lizzie.

Although life was better in South Australia, Mathes remained a quiet surly child who hid the horrors of his early Wendish childhood deep within. Losing his father at sea, when it seemed a new and better life was so close at hand, made it appear there was a curse on them for trying to escape. He became obsessed and comforted by the stories in the green book that his sister and their Aunt Katie-Lizzie read to him; stories read each evening around the fire when it was cold, or out on the verandah during the warmer months. The family also carried with them a stock of Wendish folktales as frightening as the fairytales in the book.

Aunt Giscelia believed that life in Germany had been as

brutal as the fairytales and that they should put the past behind them and make the best of their new South Australian home. Mathes, however, insisted she read him more stories from the book, or tell him Wendish tales they knew. Although clearly disturbed by the regular nightmares he suffered, he gained strange comfort from tales of the forests and creatures of the night such as wolves and bats, tales of changelings and heroes, kings, princes and princesses. Aunt would forbid the fairytales some mornings after his nightmares, but come the next night he would refuse to settle until told a story. And so each night Giscelia or Aunt Katie-Lizzie continued the storytelling.

I felt that by my telling the life of my father as he used to tell it, together with stories my Aunt Giscelia told me, Sister Kathleen would understand something about German–Wendish families living in a harsh and isolated South Australian environment. Sister Kathleen rarely interrupted. She sat quietly and took over my knitting so that I could give attention to storytelling. I told my stories as though reading them from a book, and Sister Kathleen listened to every word while the knitting needles clicked in time to the rhythm of my voice.

When I reached the point in my story when Father and Aunt Giscelia reached South Australia, Sister Kathleen was so relieved that she went off to find a jug of cold water. Pouring out a tumbler of water and then passing it to me she said, 'My goodness, what a start to a new life in South Australia. I wondered who was actually going to be left alive to disembark from the ship. Are you sure you are telling me the truth, Mary?'

'Well of course, Sister, his life gets better. But as you will hear, he still had difficulties to overcome during his schooldays. Aunt Giscelia and Katie-Lizzie – who we now referred to as our grandmother – told me the next part of Father's life when I was a teenager. It will give you an understanding of what Father had to put up with being Wendish and this may help to explain why he was the way he was. But none of what

I tell you will ever excuse the way he treated our family with such brutality.'

'Oh, Mary, no one can be that brutal.'

'You have no idea, Sister.'

'You can tell me the next part of the story when I come by tomorrow afternoon. I have to go now as Matron is planning to give us a talk. I won't be able to sleep tonight though. I'll be having my own nightmares of wolves and being swept overboard. As you say, Mary, it is hard to believe. But like a frightening fairytale I can't wait to hear what's next.'

3

The next part of Mathes' life was told in several sessions for Sister Kathleen was not able to spend more than ten minutes at a time with me over the next few days. I had gathered bits and pieces over the years about Father growing up. Sometimes as we sat around the table in the evening Aunt Giscelia and my grandparents and other relatives brought up incidents that had happened to Father.

The next time Sister Kathleen could stay with me for some time I asked her to tell me a little about herself.

'Why did you become a nurse?' I asked her.

'I thought you might ask that question. My mother's sister, my Auntie Vera, married into a German family. My uncle's grandfather was a well-known doctor in the Barossa Valley. When I was a little girl, my uncle used to tell me and my brother and sister tales about his grandfather who mended bones or cut them off, or made limbs to replace them. Gory really, but we loved to hear them. Uncle's grandfather was quite famous in his day.'

'You're a quiet one. Tell me more.' I was curious to know the story of this kind woman who had taken an interest in my life.

'I will, I promise I will, but I'm not here for long today and I'd really like to hear about your father.'

'All right, but you're not going to have it all your own way, you know, Sister.' And I began the story of how my father was turned into a bully, the way Grandpa Herman had told me.

After such harrowing early years, life settled down somewhat for Mathes in Blumberg, South Australia. But it was not always easy for Mathes. Aunt Katie-Lizzie was kind and loving but Uncle Herman could be overly stern. He was extra hard on Mathes because he didn't want to be seen to raise a weak boy.

Perhaps it was also because Mathes was not his son. Already haunted by experiences in his early life, this austere treatment made Mathes forever on his guard, stern, secretive and possessive. Aunt Giscelia recalled that Mathes also suffered at school. Being bigger and older, Giscelia walked him home to protect him from the bullying of the older boys. Small for his age and with a heavy German accent, he was fair game to the Australian lads who lay in wait for him as he made his way home from school.

Until Aunt Giscelia offered protection, the local non-German lads made his life a misery by calling him 'sissy', 'cry-baby', 'midget' and, like many Germans, 'kraut' after sauerkraut, the cabbage dish and staple diet of German families. Aunt Giscelia believed he should have made friends with other German lads, but as he hadn't he eventually fought his own battles.

Uncle Herman thought it was unhealthy for a boy to have few or no friends to play with. No one realised that as Mathes was required to work each day after school and on Saturday mornings for Herman in the family general store, it left Mathes not only overworked but with little time to form friendships. Herman made sure that Mathes was involved in the local Lutheran church, not just as part of the congregation, but doing odd jobs for the pastor. This responsibility gave him confidence and respect from the pastor and his little band of helpers, the handymen, the cleaners and the women who did the flowers. Mathes took pride in his role of caring for the church. All may have continued smoothly but for the night a gang of bully-boys broke into the church, smashing vases and violating the sacred place. The fourteen-year-old Mathes was blamed for not locking the main door and lost his voluntary role at the church, bringing him shame and humiliation. Herman knew how particular Mathes was about locking up the church and he didn't like to see him suffer from the cowardly act of others. He devised a plan, telling Mathes, 'Don't worry, lad, we'll catch them at their own game. It's the harvest festival next week and I believe those hooligans will be back to pinch the offerings. You and I will spread about town the kind of offerings that will be on show in the church, and make it the best display yet. They won't be able to resist, and we'll be ready for them.'

Herman told Mathes that he was going to arrange a special surprise for the boys. He arranged a display of wheat sheaves around the base of a large circular table which had a cane basket filled with hundreds of brightly painted boiled eggs as a centrepiece. He believed these boys who liked to make as much mess as possible would head first to the highly decorated eggs and have fun throwing them about the church.

Herman told no one of the plan other than Mathes. The pastor would never allow the use of a cruel trap in his church. Herman made sure he was last to leave church that Friday evening when members of the congregation met to arrange the harvest festival display. When the display was completed and they began leaving the church, Herman lingered. As the little group of helpers passed through the door Herman slipped a large dingo trap from his sack. He quickly set the murderous trap and shoved it beneath a thick layer of straw under the display table, believing that catching the vandals was worth the risk.

When Herman and Mathes returned early in the morning before the others they were alarmed at what they found. The door had been left open but fortunately the display was intact and no damage had been done in the church. But many of the wheat stalks were soaked in blood and had to be replaced. Herman was worried about the degree of injury.

No one told the true story, it would amount to a confession of ransacking the church. The boy caught in the cruel trap lied to his parents after he hobbled home with his friends, saying he had been caught in a trap laid in a creek bed, not the Lutheran

Church. Many such traps were laid about in the countryside for wild dogs and rabbits. Only Mathes and his Uncle Herman knew the truth.

The boys involved stuck to their story of the injury having taken place in a creek bed. The boy's leg had been seriously mutilated and needed emergency treatment from the local doctor. It took months for it to heal and the boy walked with a limp from that time onwards.

This incident was a turning point in Mathes Schippan's life. The church was not vandalised again and other boys kept well away from him, for the real story of how the boy was injured was known among the vandals and their friends. Mathes was eventually once again offered his voluntary job at the church. After the incident, he was given a new kind of respect that he had to live up to. It gave him a sense of being in charge. The boys of the township knew that while he was quiet and kept to himself, he was someone you didn't fool around with. No one took advantage of him again. It was from this time that Mathes' nightmares stopped.

With this new-found confidence, Mathes learned when to throw his weight about and became a bully himself. This period coincided with him suddenly transforming from a puny boy to a big and brutish young man, like many lads who worked the land. With the little spare time he could find, he threw himself into farm work for a local farmer, removing any possibility of meeting other young men his age. He was unconcerned; it was this work that would eventually help him buy his own farm. And wasn't that what every young man working on the land wanted for himself?

When I finished this part of the story Sister Kathleen said, 'You don't realise how hard it can be for some boys growing up. You hear about boys bullying smaller ones, and after hearing your story I can't help feeling some sympathy for your father.'

'That may be so. But when you see what he became, you won't have any sympathy left for him.'

'Oh, Mary. Your father must have had something good about him when your mother married him. Maybe tomorrow or when I have a bit more time you can tell me about them – how they met and what the Towitta house looked like. I have to go now and organise the stripping of the beds in one of the main wards.'

# 4

When Sister Kathleen left I thought about what I had been told about the time my mother and father married. Johanne was quiet and demure and lived in the same township. She was not known as a beauty, but she was more than a suitable wife for a farmer with prospects. She was of good farming stock, hardworking and had good childbearing hips. There was some muttering in the township because Johanne was more than six years older than Mathes – crueller tongues said it was more like ten. There were those who thought she was well past childbearing age. Mathes married my mother when she was three months short of her thirty-fifth birthday. Like me, she had been a domestic servant. But unlike me, she worked in her position for over ten years for a local doctor in Blumberg. What she may have lacked in looks, she made up for in bearing a brood of seven children.

Some time before Johanne and Mathes were married, he moved down the hill to the drier lands on the Murray River Flats where he bought 150 acres of open flat land on a credit lease. It was 1888, fifteen long years, before he could say the farm was his. I was eleven years old when Father proudly announced he had freehold ownership. Their farm was over a mile from the little township of Towitta, named after the nearby reedy creek. It flowed in winter but its natural springs bubbled just below the surface and could be found in the heat of the summer when the creek was bone dry. The creek was like an oasis in the middle of the bleak red plains. It was full of giant river red gums and mallee trees that were home to flocks of green ring-neck parrots, galahs, magpies and other birds made homeless by the clearing of land to grow wheat and barley.

When Mathes built the farmhouse, he said it was like the thatched house in Germany, only bigger. It couldn't have been much bigger. Even with the extra room tacked onto the kitchen end, the place was still small. Father said he could remember the floor plan and the thick thatch of the house in Germany as though it was yesterday. The first thing he did when he moved onto his land was to knock up a small wooden paling barn while he lived in a tent. He then lived in the barn while building the farmhouse. When he finished the stone structure with its walls more than six inches thick, it was thatched to make a roof a foot thick. Although the house was long and narrow, measuring thirty feet in length when completed, it was barely eleven feet wide. The pantry and storeroom were built onto the house after August was born and when I was about six years old. You could only enter this attached room from outside the house. It was the same length as the kitchen, but narrower. The addition made the entire length of the house forty feet.

Just before the roof was thatched, Mathes married Johanne in Eden Valley and took her back to live in the unroofed farmhouse. Their plans to start married life in the house were ruined when the heavens opened up on the first night and came down in a deluge. Johanne used to say that was an ill omen. Instead of living in the unroofed farmhouse, they had to be content to spend their first few weeks together camping in the barn while the thatching was undertaken between the rain showers by a German thatcher from Sedan.

The farmhouse had no ceilings. It remained open to the rafters and the straw thatch. The rafters, cut from the native pine forest in the foothills, were, as Mathes kept reminding them, 'of the finest native pine and perfectly straight'. Johanne often muttered how a house was not completed until its ceilings were installed. She never raised enough money from her meagre housekeeping allowance to make the temporary ceilings from calico that she hoped. Most people used calico or hessian cloth to catch the many insects and other creatures that flopped down from the rafters when you least expected it.

The lack of a calico or hessian ceiling caused my sister,

Pauline, and me many a fright in the middle of the night. With us already tense after a frightening story, the fall of a large insect, mouse, possum, bat – or even a rat – onto to us in bed periodically caused us to scream in fright.

The front door into the kitchen, that rattled and banged when it was windy, was fastened at night by a large iron bolt but was rarely locked, even though most of us were worried to death at what could come in. When it rattled it took all of mine or Pauline's bravado to climb out of bed and stuff old rags in the gaps to muffle the sounds. This was not before we argued as to whose turn it was to climb out of bed and do it.

The house was white-washed by the brothers. They did this task each spring as soon as the eldest one was old enough to hold a paintbrush. Although the outside walls were built of stone, Mathes had built the house as one big room, adding the internal wattle and daub walls afterwards. The front door opened into the main room that was a third of the size of the main house and combined the kitchen and living room. Off it was mine and Pauline's bedroom, which you had to walk through to reach our parents' room. So there were three rooms in a row, and a small separate room alongside the kitchen that, as I said, was entered from outside and not part of the living area.

Dominating the main room was the oversized whitewashed fireplace and chimney breast made from large stones collected from the paddocks and the nearby creek beds. Big, black iron pots hung down from chains and hooks that were attached inside the chimney. The floors were simply of rock-solid dirt that was buffed up to shine like glass from the continual spillage of animal fats and the blood and tallow that was deliberately poured onto the surface.

Each room had the tiniest of windows. Only three feet high by about eighteen inches wide, each one made up of two panes of glass, one over the other. The windows were hinged at the frame halfway down, dividing the two panes which could revolve on a windy day like a windmill if not properly fastened.

According to Mother, when building, our father had given no thought to the size the house should have been. It seemed to shrink with the arrival of each new baby and as we seven Schippan children grew up and crowded the place. He intended adding another bedroom to the house and buying Mother new pieces of furniture but our growing family and our poor financial state put paid to any good intentions. We shared the same poor state as most of our neighbours.

A shortage of money due to ongoing drought conditions and a new baby every other year or so, meant there were only a few sticks of furniture. For a few years we four older children were crammed into the middle room, while Mother and Father slept in the kitchen-living-room area and the three smallest children, August, Will and Bertha, slept in the furthest room from the kitchen.

The house heated up quickly and was a hot box in the summer but snug and warm in the winter. On the hottest summer nights the family moved outside to sleep under the stars despite being at the mercy of the buzzing, biting mosquitoes. It was after one hot summer night that ended in a sudden downpour, that the brothers took shelter in the small barn. From that night all four brothers slept there. For the rest of the family, it was a blessed relief. Mother and Father with Bertha claimed the farthest room as their bedroom while Pauline and I slept in the middle room.

Towitta was a windy, bleak township with its howling, moaning and sighs that constantly brought to my mind old Wendish witches slinking about, clawing their way through the gaps between door and window crevices, bringing with them red dust. So deep was it at times that the women spent hours shovelling it outdoors. The contents of drawers and cupboards were often taken outside and shaken free of the curse of the red dust. Even in those rare periods when there wasn't a breath of wind for weeks at a time, the dust still crept in.

The dogged determination of local farmers around Towitta to clear the land of anything that didn't resemble a wheat or barley stalk saw much of the dense mallee landscape vanish. I believed this was why there was so much dust. Local farmers were stubborn and refused to believe this, defiantly continuing to clear the land for crops. The mallee roots from the piles of dead trees were the perfect fuel during the winter. And Father built several stock paddocks with walls made entirely of mallee roots. So the wood had its uses, but the chronic dust problem made me realise how more pleasant it might have been had more of the old mallee scrub been left growing to anchor the soil, as windbreaks and for shade for the grazing stock.

The years of living in such a lonely place sharpened my nose to the changing scents of the breezes throughout the year. In the summer the hint of eucalyptus would reach me as the wind blew down from the hilly wooded areas around Mount Pleasant. Towards the end of winter the scent of the canary yellow wattles wafted in. After I met Gustave, a waft of heady wattles took me back to our private times together. The smells of winter included farmyard smells of pigs and sheep, and sometimes wet ripe manure after a rare rain. On even rarer occasions the eerie fog that settled over the River Murray miles away, reached us cold and dank. The river swamps, our grandparents recalled, smelled like the bottom of a German village pond.

At Towitta you could smell rain twenty minutes before it arrived for the air would have a strong spicy fragrance of damp earth mixed with flower smells. This always gave me time to run and pull clothes from the clothes line made of barbed wire stretched between two native pine poles. Father made it this way because he thought the strongest winds could not blow away clothes secured to the barbs. However, if the wind hadn't managed to blow all the clothes off the line they were often ruined by the barbarous spikes. When they were blown away countless hours were spent searching the paddocks for the missing clothes that we could not afford to lose. Sometimes after a big blow they were never seen again.

Sometimes when I was hanging out the washing or feeding poultry, a whiff of some far-off scent such as sandalwood would fill the air as the wind blew. I often wondered where some of the scents had blown from, and closed my eyes and wished I could be there, anywhere as long as it was as far away from Towitta and Father as possible.

After the remains of our family moved to Light's Pass I often sat in a field of waving grass or corn, remembering the times I saw the sea when I lived in Adelaide. Even now in the bleak confines of the Consumptive Home I often dream of seeing the sparkle on the sea in the way that I first saw it one early spring morning. It glinted like silver paper and the salty smell was strong on that Sunday morning when Rebekah, the friend I worked with, and I took the train to Semaphore. In the spring when the meadow grass is at its longest, I would sit on a small hill at Light's Pass and watch it waving in the wind until it became the waves on the sea. That's how I travelled in my mind to the edge of the world and escaped my life.

# 5

Just after our midday meal the next day, Sister Kathleen rushed in to say she could spend half an hour with me as she was between chores and the matron had gone home early feeling unwell. She took my arm and walked me out to the verandah where we found a sheltered spot away from the breeze that was making sitting outside unpleasant.

'Sit here, Mary,' she said, patting a cushioned chair. 'I'll sit over here so I can see what's going on. I may have to suddenly leave you when someone discovers I'm missing. Yesterday you were going to tell me about living in a Wendish home in that lonely place and what made it different from mine.'

You'd have noticed the difference the moment you stepped inside the kitchen of our house. From Aunt Giscelia and Mother, Pauline and I learned about our ancestors – including our adopted grandparents – who came from Upper Saxony in the Fatherland. My father preferred his mother tongue of Wendish, which he spoke at home or when he was in company with his sister, Giscelia, and my grandparents. When Pauline and I stayed with Aunt Giscelia and her family, especially when we were young girls, we would talk solely in this strange language. Like Father, we also told Wendish folktales and sang the songs we knew. Aunt Giscelia had a voice like a songbird and sang solo in church, or at home when they had spinning evenings. We were constantly reminded of our grandfather's loss at sea, because he had been a troubadour with a fine voice before he settled down to a forester's life.

Whereas in Germany spinning was with flax, the tradition was adapted and continued in South Australia by spinning wool instead. Aunt Giscelia was the local *Kantorka*, leading the singing and teaching others the many songs she knew. She took over the role from Katie-Lizzie, her aunt. I was sure she never reached the end of her huge stock of songs for we always seemed to be learning new ones. It was these 'foreign ways' that made us different, but we would not relinquish them. We continued to cook in our own way, to tat, crochet, knit, sew, spin, weave, sing and paint hard-boiled eggs at Easter. We loved to hear the old family songs that were laments about lost love or nature.

It was through folktales that our hopes and desires took root. At night Pauline and I would tell each other stories that included dwarfs, dragons and other nightmare-inducing creatures. One of the scariest creatures of all was the waterman, or in Wendish, the *wodny muz*, who lurked outside the house waiting to entice us into the massive underground water tank or some other forbidding watery place. Fortunately, some of the more frightening tales involving this creature who wished to lure children to watery graves couldn't happen in Towitta through lack of water. Despite this, Mother was in constant fear that we'd drown in the water tank even though it was kept covered with corrugated iron. We had no need to fear rain, rivers or lakes, but we were terrified of the water tank, a death trap, and the place where horrible creatures of the night lurked. We laughed and gasped but the thrill of being alive when so many of the fairytale characters had been killed, stayed with us long after the story was told.

On wild nights when the wind moaned and howled around the farm, I might whisper, 'Watch out, Pauline Schippan, I can hear the Noon Lady coming, she's coming to get *you*.'

This witch, the Noon Lady, also known as the Woman of Midday or *Mittagsfrau*, was very much like the *wodny muz* or the *Ztynjedobry* who also harmed children and babies in horrible ways. It was well known by Wends that when a small child wandered into the bush and disappeared, the horrible witch had stolen the child for herself. As far as we were concerned, it was pointless setting a black tracker onto the trail of a missing child. You couldn't escape the witch's power if she had her evil eye on you. Even when she didn't actually take a child she'd leave little signs of her visits. Freckles were stamped on the uncovered parts of a child's body when their parents turned away for a moment. Pauline and I couldn't ignore this witch for we witnessed an event caused by her evil when we were young.

Sister Kathleen interrupted to ask, 'This is the truth, Mary?'
I looked at her, 'Would I make it up?'

All Wendish children know she takes babies away if they are neglected or not baptised immediately after birth. Although my parents had seven children, I know there had been another baby and when I was about nine it was taken away by the witch and replaced with a changeling. I remembered Mother cried a lot, she kept asking Father if the Noon Lady would strike again. Pauline and I heard snatches of conversation, mainly in hushed but anguished tones and whispers between the aunts long after the event. I heard Father curse the witch, telling Mother, 'It won't happen again if we're careful.'

From what I could make out the Noon Lady had done a swap and left her with a 'no good' creature – half animal, half human, with a big head and swollen belly, that would never live a normal life – a changeling. Mother wept, 'Oh my poor little baby, where has she taken you?'

But we knew. We stood rigid with fear watching Father pick up the writhing tiny creature and run with it from the house on what was a rare stormy night. I can remember clutching Pauline's hand and I couldn't take my head out of her apron, I was terrified. But Pauline was so fascinated that she dragged me to the kitchen door and outside where we saw Father take this monstrous-looking creature out into a paddock, scattering and startling a large mob of emus that gathered around the farm when food and water were scarce. We watched him put down his oil lamp and drop the squirming changeling on the ground next to it and then he killed it with a spade, shoving the blade through its neck.

We were shocked. Pauline dragged me back inside. I still can't quite believe what I saw. I suppose Father must have buried it somewhere so that only he knew of its whereabouts. By this time, Pauline and I were sitting together on the sofa. I wouldn't let go of her hand. When Father returned, he looked wild and murderous. He didn't utter a word but rushed to retrieve the family Bible and we all cowered and trembled while he sat at the table leafing through the pages for relevant passages. He then ranted, loud and menacingly. All the time Mother was wailing with grief in the bedroom. It was a pitiful sound and of course it set us crying hysterically, for I thought Father might take one of us out there next, especially if we were to disobey him. As if this wasn't bad enough, I can remember the angry-sounding emus had positioned themselves outside the house making their dreadful drumming sounds from deep in their throats while tapping on the windows with their beaks. I thought of the evil eye as they tapped and stared in at us with their piercing eyes.

Sister Kathleen leaned over to me and took my hand, 'You've lived with that all your life, Mary? I can't believe that anyone could behave that way. That was murder what your father did.'

She paused to draw breath, then asked, 'Did your mother really believe that stuff about the witch?'

'Oh, Sister, but of course she did. We all did. We still do.'

I told her all my sleep problems dated from this violent event and that I began to have terrifying nightmares where I would wake each night and feel a heavy weight on my chest. As I struggled to see what caused it I spied a stunted goblin type monster sitting on me – the changeling perhaps. Even when it moved from my chest to the corner of the bedroom I was totally paralysed with fear.

Sister Kathleen didn't know what to say at first. She shook her head in disbelief and walked around the verandah adjusting her cap. Then she said, 'I've heard about this type of nightmare but I never knew people really had them. I thought they only happened in books. I just don't know what to say, but I won't be able to sleep now. Mary, I know you are a good storyteller, but I know you didn't make this up. I'm sorry, I have to go now, and it's my day off tomorrow. I'll be back as soon as I can.'

She led me back to my room and gave me a reassuring pat on my arm before leaving me.

## 6

A few evenings later, Sister Kathleen called by before going on night duty. She found me sitting in my room knitting the tiny baby clothes that kept me busy. She drew up the spare chair, 'Seeing you with those tiny booties, Mary, reminds me that we haven't spoken about the baby in your family, your youngest sister, Bertha. Can you tell me about her? I've heard bits and pieces, but I am curious to know what she was like. They say she was a very pretty girl.'

'You'd best sit down and make yourself comfortable while I think a moment or two how best to tell you about her.' And soon I began.

When Pauline and I first shared the three-quarter iron bedstead, Bertha, being the youngest, slept in Mother's room on a makeshift bed. The situation changed when I went to work in Adelaide.

Bertha was a thorn in my side from the time she was born when I was ten-and-a-half years old. Father insisted she be named after Mother, Johanne Elizabeth, but she was always called Bertha. Pauline was the eldest, twelve-and-a-half years of age at that time. After me there followed a tribe of four brothers ranging from nine down to two years of age. There was no chance to catch one's breath or have a moment of peace with the work they made for Pauline and me. They were demanding, always hungry, grubby and naughty. From the time Mother thought we were capable, Pauline and I were placed in charge of looking after them. Although it was hard work, Mother was fair in her expectations of us. But this all changed with the arrival of Bertha.

Bertha was completely different to August and Willy who were different again from the older brothers, Frederick and

Heinrich. And she was nothing like Pauline or me. She was the odd one in the family, a real spitfire who liked having fun by playing tricks or teasing her brothers to get her own back for terrifying her. Her fiery temper matched Father's and my own. Being the baby of the family, she was treated as one and got away with murder. When I returned from Adelaide I spoke to her in English, while speaking to Mother and Father in a mixture of German and Wendish. She wanted to be a school-teacher when she left school so it was important for her to speak English fluently. I helped her where possible. My two years in Adelaide had greatly improved my spoken English, but I still couldn't read or write very well. Bertha was the smartest, too big and cocky for her own boots in our family. She took the most risks and regularly tested Father's authority.

When she was born after a crop of grubby boys, Mother drooled over her new baby love. Until Bertha's arrival, Pauline as first born and first daughter, was Mother's favourite. I couldn't help feeling jealous. Yet Pauline, who had more reason than me to feel jealous of the newest baby, was long-suffering and never complained. Pauline had room in her heart for all of us and if she felt the new baby had now become Mother's favourite, she never showed it. If anything, she added to the spoiling of Bertha and loved her like her own. But I never did.

Speaking of Bertha brought back so many mixed thoughts. 'It is so difficult to speak about her. You have no idea how much trouble she caused in the family. Although she was my sister, I can't say I showed her sisterly love.'

Sister Kathleen asked gently, 'Would you like to call it a night? I can see you are tired.'

'No, it's all right. I want to continue as I need to cleanse myself of these memories. I've carried it around for far too long.

When we should have been at school, Mother often kept Pauline and me at home to help with the never-ending laundry, cleaning, patching of worn-out clothes and preparation of food. Apart from this, we ran round after the boys changing their clothes, wiping their dirty faces and hands and feeding them. They were like naughty puppies.

As if this wasn't enough, Bertha was different. She grew up spoilt, disobedient and sneaky. If she cried she was nursed, if not by Mother, certainly by Pauline. When she demanded food, she was fed there and then. Whatever she wanted, she was given. While the rest of us were familiar with the sting of Mother's hand or Father's flicking whip for minor crimes, Bertha did not suffer these punishments. And while Mother spent hours besotted by the cute baby, we were given more chores. Whereas we whacked the boys if they misbehaved, smacking Bertha risked a clout from Mother, who reminded us, 'I've told you before, I'll deal with Bertha.'

Nothing was straightforward with Bertha. Pauline knew how to manage her, but I didn't. She interfered in the brief amount of time I could have to myself. When I tried to sneak away for a lone walk along the nearby lane towards the creek, Mother would know and before I had walked far I'd hear her shouting, 'If you're going for a walk, take Bertha with you.'

I'd reply, 'Do I have too? It's not fair. I just want to get away from her so I can be on my own for a while.' I'd grumble with disbelief and irritation, but it was pointless disobeying for if I did so, I'd be forbidden to take a walk. Then she'd skip and run about me as we headed down the track, and chatter, chatter, chatter. All I wanted was a few minutes of peace now and again, but this was difficult when Bertha demanded my attention.

Apart from looking after the brothers or Bertha, we were given specific chores from an early age, and Father ensured we completed them. I looked after the pigs and the two cows while Pauline was responsible for the poultry and most of the cooking. Life on our farm was one of hard work and dreary routine. Father made sure we were never idle. We livened our existences any way we could and visitors were seen as a welcome diversion. However, not all were welcomed by Father.

And so I began the story of Mr Khan, the Afghan hawker.

$$\approx\!\!\!\!\!\sim \quad 7 \quad \sim\!\!\!\!\!\approx$$

Father never liked hawkers or travelling salesmen calling in at the farm. We believed this was because he was ashamed of our poor state. We looked forward to these colourful visitors because they distracted us from the gruelling and tedious farm chores and the feeling of isolation. Mother liked these visitors too and sometimes bought a comb, a new pair of scissors, cloth, ribbons or some miracle potion such as Sea Foam, a pink mixture that we were told cured anything and everything. The hawkers brought colourful wares for us to see and showed little knick-knacks and baubles that women liked, especially women so far from city shops. As the hawkers declared themselves fortune tellers as well, this was an added treat when Father was well away. We were eager to know what the future held in store for us. In our dull lives, they gave us hope by telling us our fortunes.

These travellers called often until Father suddenly took exception to one of the Afghan hawkers. Because of the heat and dust in summertime, and the long journeys between stops, Mother always offered a traveller a cool drink of water or some morsel that might be available. But one such day Father had cross words with Mr Khan, one of the hawkers, because Father believed he had been overly familiar with Pauline. Father saw their behaviour as flirting, and flirting as loose and immoral behaviour, especially if one of his own daughters was involved.

Mr Khan was tall and handsome, with sea-green eyes, and he cut a romantic figure in his flowing white robes, saffron turban and long black waistcoat. It was difficult to know how old he was for his black beard hid most of his face. From his white teeth and the slight crow's-foot wrinkles around his smiling eyes, I thought he must be only in his early thirties, an ideal age for Pauline. My eyes often lingered on him too, and when our eyes met, I was charmed.

We had become friendly with Mr Khan over a period of time, a man not only cannily informed but so charming. He would display lovely cloth, pointing out how it matched our eyes or our hair. One time he held red ribbon up to my hair, and I was left wondering what he meant when he called me a butterfly and put his hands together to copy the actions of the flitting creature. Mother put her hand to her mouth and gave me a worried look. I thought it an innocent comment and laughed. I asked him, 'Mr Khan, whom will I marry?'

Shaking his head he responded, as he always did, 'Sorry, Missy, I cannot tell you.' I noticed he couldn't answer my sisters' questions on this most important topic either. This was the one and only piece of information we were really interested in. Yet he never answered.

On the day Mr Khan was brazenly flirting with Pauline while showing her pretty ribbons, he had forgotten to tie up his hungry horse which wandered, complete with cart, into one of the barns where our meagre hay supplies were stored. It was there that father found the hungry animal tucking in for a feed and removed the horse by grabbing the reins and pressing down on the bit. Mr Khan was run off the farm at gunpoint. We were dismayed at Father's violent outburst. We couldn't understand his behaviour. Mother explained, 'Your father is worried that the hawker will take Pauline away. He remembers what happened to his mother.'

Mr Khan's visit that day didn't end the matter for Father continued to curse and shout at him whenever they met on the road. Not long after, Frederick was returning from Sedan one afternoon when he saw Father and the Afghan feuding on the track leading to the farm. Father blocked Mr Khan's way and was trying to force him to turn back by aiming a shotgun at him. When Frederick arrived, Father retracted the terrible weapon and the hawker turned back. Father shouted after him, 'Keep away from my womenfolk, or else.'

Four weeks later, about the time we next expected him to

visit, Mr Khan was found dead with a fractured skull on the roadside near Sedan. It was decided at the inquest that he must have fallen from his wagon, there was no other explanation for the blow to his head. The weal on his arm and across his face, however, couldn't be explained. But we all knew Father was fond of using his whip.

When we heard of Mr Khan's death we were horrified and Pauline wept uncontrollably. I was rather surprised at this outpouring of sorrow and it made me suspicious something else had been going on. Mother kept telling the distraught Pauline to pull herself together, telling her, 'My girl, he was only a hawker and you didn't really know him, a foreigner, not even a Christian.'

Such remarks failed to comfort Pauline. She would fly out of the door and into the paddock where she sobbed all the louder. Mother never told Father the reason why Pauline was always crying, she kept inventing other excuses such as her favourite lamb dying. We talked of Mr Khan's death between ourselves for months afterwards, but whenever Father was present we remained silent. We wondered why he refused to discuss the death. After all, Father was always free with his opinions and advice, yet when Mr Khan was concerned, Father remained silent.

Frederick also had his suspicions, telling us, 'I know Father has something to do with this.'

Mother was shocked, 'How can you accuse your father of such a terrible crime?'

'Mother, you weren't there that day. When I came across them on the roadway, Father was pointing the gun right in Mr Khan's face and shouting at him to keep away from his daughters. Mr Khan just sat there bravely, refusing to defend himself, or budge.'

'But that doesn't prove anything,' Mother answered.

'Father threatened to thrash him. What are we to believe? And rumours abound at the pub.'

Startled, Mother asked, 'Since when have you been going to the pub?'

'I don't, my friends go there and they told me. They've been asking me questions about Father. They all know that he treats us harshly and sometimes whips us. And Mr Khan had unexplained whip welts on him.'

'Surely not, son? Who is spreading such wicked rumours about what goes on in this house? What business is it of theirs?'

'I'm sure no one is at all interested what goes on here normally, but when such things as unexplained deaths happen in this sleepy district, people will question anybody to get the answers they want. Look, I plan to leave here when I find a position on a cattle station up north. I'm not willing to put up with his whip and temper any longer. And if I can't find a situation soon, I'll go and live with Grandpa at Eden Valley. They've told me I can go there any time.'

Mother put her hand to her mouth and gasped with dismay when Frederick reminded her that family matters such as Father's brutality were discussed, just as was everyone else's business in Towitta and Sedan.

For weeks after Mr Khan's death, Father was edgy and barely spoke, not even to Mother. Surely Father wouldn't be so stupid as to murder an innocent hawker. The inquest findings declared it a tragic accident, but each night after we went to bed we would discuss it as a murder, for that's what we believed it to be.

Pauline was more affected by his death than the rest of us. It seemed to trigger off some deep-held fears about our own situation, of our isolation on a dusty farm. Each day she spoke of her wish to be rescued by some young man passing through, someone like Mr Khan. She was older than me and her chances of marriage were slipping away, as were Mother's when she married Father. After Mr Khan's suspicious death, our storytelling included new tales of Arabian sheiks riding frisky white Arab stallions who rescued fair maidens from imprisonment.

We shared our fantasies about Mr Khan, that he was really a sheik. Pauline told me she should have run away with him when she had the chance.

Not long after, Pauline fell sick with tuberculosis. During her fevers she fantasised about what could have been between her and the handsome Afghan. The doctor told Mother that such fantasies were part of the condition. He also told us she could have fits and have unusually strong feelings towards men.

Pauline made sure we did not forget Mr Khan, and she convinced us about Father's involvement in his death. Despite the chronic illness that made Pauline weak, she found the energy to be a good hater of Father. She blocked him from her life by avoiding him and never talking with him unless it was necessary. Mother was the natural buffer between us and Father. She soothed many blazing outbursts of blame and criticism.

At this point Sister Kathleen said she didn't want to hear any more of the story that evening for she was upset about the handsome and innocent Mr Khan. When I said I had more to tell her about Father and his violence she said she didn't want to hear any more for now, she needed time think about what I'd told her. It was nearly a week before she came to see me again. I hadn't seen her around the hospital and I thought maybe she was avoiding me, but she told me she had been ill for several days. She also told me she couldn't stop thinking about my family having to live with Father's violence, and that the story about the charming Mr Khan had so upset her that it made her cry as though she'd known him herself.

'Honestly, Mary, I think if I'd been there, I'd have taken the shotgun to your father myself.'

'I can tell you, there was never a day I didn't have those feelings. But you think these things, you never carry them out.'

## 8

When we sat down to talk, I asked if she felt strong enough to listen to more of the story that followed Mr Khan's death, for she was still clearly upset by what I had told her.

'Of course I want to hear the story, all of it. When I went home last week I felt very sad about the Afghan hawker you spoke about and it took days to get over it. But I am ready.'

I was curious, 'Where is home exactly?'

'I go home to Angaston on the train when I have several days off together. That's where my mother and father live. My father used to be a publican there, but since he's retired, they live on the edge of the town where they raise poultry and a few animals.'

'When you went home, did you tell them about me?'

'Not Father, but I did tell Mother when we were alone. After you told me about Mr Khan I had to talk about it. I was very upset about that, Mary.'

'I wish you hadn't but I understand your need to share this sad story. What does she think about you knowing me?'

'She told me to be careful.'

We looked at each other and laughed.

'Really … '

'Yes, but I told her you were very sick and you had no strength to raise a carving knife to me.'

Again we shared laughter, the mood was almost lighthearted as I continued.

Not long after Mr Khan's death, Father demonstrated a serious act of violence on a neighbour's farm. It took place during a child's birthday party at Mr Blenkiron's house, less than half a mile from our house. I was invited to go with Bertha, August and Willy and while we were enjoying the party one Sunday afternoon, several Sedan lads appeared uninvited and started disturbing the peace by throwing stones onto the roof of the house and howling like wolves. It transpired that one of them hadn't taken kindly to being rejected by one of Mr Blenkiron's attractive daughters and wanted revenge of a sort. They went around Mr Blenkiron's property rattling the fences and shed doors, banging them with their long sticks, like a drum.

The gang was made up of Carl and Hermann Hartwig and their chums the three Radomi brothers. Their noisy behaviour frightened Mrs Blenkiron and terrified the younger children who ran indoors crying. When Mr Blenkiron strode out and faced the boys, shouting at them to go home, they laughed and jeered at him and threw a mass of little stones at the windows of his house. The gang of boys were well-known troublemakers in the district. They pulled up noticeboards, and removed and opened gates to let stock run loose. They rode recklessly through the streets of Sedan on half-wild horses churning up clouds of red dust. No one seemed able to stop their behaviour.

To start with we were pleased that Father could put his violent temper to good use to protect us all. But when he took the matter into his own hands, he went too far. The whole matter ran out of control and much to our horror ended up in the Adelaide Supreme Court.

One of the boys at the party crept out the back door of the farmhouse and ran over to our farm begging Father to come and help sort out the situation. He grabbed his loaded rifle and hurried over. When he stood in front of the larrikins they laughed in his face and threw bigger rocks. One thrown by Carl Hartwig hit Father on the side of his head and instantly drew blood. He never flinched as the blood streamed over his face and beard, but marched to one of the boys and poked him with the barrel of the rifle. When one of the boys ran to his brother's rescue, Father told them, 'If you don't leave I will fire.'

One of the other boys dared him, 'Fire away then, old man.' So Father did.

Although he fired at the ground to frighten them, the ground was so hard that the bullet ricocheted and hit Carl Hartwig in the leg. He fell to the ground groaning and bleeding heavily. 'I've been hit, don't let me die,' he pleaded, but the four remaining boys, now frightened by the shooting, ran for their horses and galloped away. Father and Mr Blenkiron carried the still-bleeding boy onto the verandah of the house.

One of the children left to fetch Dr Pullen who came some hours later and attended the wound. But when he arrived so too did the local policeman who promptly arrested Father and took him into custody. When we went home without Father we had to explain to Mother what had happened. 'What do you mean, Father has been arrested?' she screamed, wringing her hands and then babbling unintelligibly in Wendish. She knew well enough what Father's violence was like and though it was meant to be only a threat, she admitted that this time he had gone too far and could end up in prison.

But he didn't. A month later Father appeared at the Supreme Court in Adelaide charged with having 'feloniously and unlawfully and maliciously at Towitta shot Carl Hartwig with intent to do grievous bodily harm'. Father was lucky, the judge recognised his attempts to protect a group of law-abiding citizens and was sympathetic. Nevertheless, he let him know that larrikinism must not be quelled with guns. He also stated 'it was an unlawful act to fire off a loaded gun in a struggle, and if the jury believed the facts as presented then the prisoner, although a very respectable man, had no right to fire the gun, and was guilty of unlawfully wounding'. Although the jury found Father not guilty, the judge gave him a caution. 'If Hartwig had been killed, Mr Schippan, you would be standing trial for his murder.'

Father was acquitted but he was humiliated for being arrested. He believed he had acted reasonably to protect innocent people in danger from a threatening gang. After he returned home, humiliation gave way to fury. Inevitably, he took out his rage on the elder brothers, Frederick and Heinrich.

He saw the two elder boys as friends of the gang and cruelly stepped up his tyranny over them. He tormented them, delving out harsh beatings, but one day when attempting to horse whip them for a minor indiscretion they turned on him and whipped him instead. Before he had recovered from the thrashing they dashed into one of the nearby wooded creeks where they hid for some days before heading to the farm of Mother's brother in Eden Valley.

But the violence did not end there. Early one January morning, a few days before I went to live in Adelaide, another hawker, Fred Struckmeyer, was found dead in Sedan. On several occasions he had risked visiting our farm after Mr Khan's death. The policeman, William Burgenmeister, found him on the roadway and believed he had been killed in a fight for his skull was crushed in as though attacked with a blunt heavy object. The findings of the inquest were different. The cause was unconfirmed, but it was believed he must have fallen from his cart and been crushed by the wheels. At the time his cart was fully laden with new stock and this would have added to its weight making it capable of crushing his head.

Sister Kathleen must have been growing accustomed to the bizarre aspects of my family stories. She looked neither shocked nor stunned but just seemed to breathe deeply and shake her head. Then she eagerly looked up, anticipating the next instalment. Whenever I suggested we should call an end to the storytelling, she pleaded with me not to stop.

'So that all happened just as you were going to live in Adelaide. My goodness, I'd have been glad to leave all that behind too. Perhaps you could tell me of what happened to you in Adelaide when I next come. It can't be for a few days, as we are short staffed because some nurses are away with this terrible flu that's going around. We have also had quite a few new patients admitted. It would not be exaggerating to call it bedlam.'

## 9

The next time Sister Kathleen came she brought me skeins of lemon-coloured wool for knitting. It was a sunny day and she took me again into a shady part of the garden to a bench under one of the large peppercorn trees. She said we probably wouldn't be disturbed there.

'And I've brought us some fruit cake to share.'

She made me comfortable with a rug over my lap before I began the story of the next part of my life spent in Adelaide as a servant to a wealthy family.

The Waters family lived in a large two-storey house in North Adelaide that overlooked the Parklands and the centre of the city. I assisted a servant named Rebekah who was two years older than me. I helped her with the laundry, general house-keeping and in the kitchen. We came from the same region and our families knew each other from church. When Mrs Waters asked Rebekah if she knew of another girl who would like a situation, Rebekah – who had been at school with Pauline – thought of me.

It was no easy matter to leave the farm even though the money I earned in Adelaide would help it survive. Father erupted into spasms of rage at Mother who he believed had plotted with Mrs Waters to arrange the job. His intention was that none of us would ever leave the farm; but for the tightening grip of the never-ending drought, I doubted that I ever would have. Mother kept reminding him just how poor we really were and the common sense of allowing me to work for this well-to-do and highly regarded Adelaide family. Father grudgingly surrendered but only from fear of offending the Waters family. And he was consoled when he learned how much I would earn and how much of that would be passed to him.

Mother had told me, 'Of course you can keep a few shillings from your wages but you will have to send us the rest, at least until matters here improve. And perhaps, Mary, you will find yourself a nice young man there.' And so I left home for Adelaide when I was almost twenty years old.

When I arrived to take up my position I was shown into Mrs Waters' parlour. 'I am very pleased that you can come and work for us, Mary, but there are some rules you need to know. Rebekah will be able to tell you of my expectations. But I need to stress that I don't wish to see you near our private living rooms unless you have good reason. You have the kitchen, the yard and your room as your territory. And it goes without saying that I expect you to work quietly and diligently.' She then led me to the room I was to share with Rebekah.

As servants we soon learnt our place. In return for this and doing our chores to the satisfaction of Mrs Waters, we expected that we would be left to work without unnecessary interference. Our reward – or our right as we saw it – was that on special occasions in the evening we could leave the house, as well as on Sundays once breakfast was over and all the chores done. We wanted no obstacle or hindrance to our work for there was so much that had to be done. Rebekah told me Mrs Waters was a fair employer, but to watch out for her beady-eyed mother-in-law who lived in the house. When scrubbing a floor she would be there, watching us. At times she would study what we were doing, complaining, 'My girl, look at what you're doing, you've missed a bit there in the corner.'

'Yes, ma'am,' I'd reply, and set to re-cleaning the floor.

Sister couldn't contain herself, 'Yes, well I know what that is like. Sometimes Matron suddenly appears out of nowhere and does the same thing. It makes you feel so small.' She paused and smiled warmly, 'I've heard that some of the larger Adelaide villas are very beautiful inside. What was the one like that you lived in, Mary?'

Although Adelaide had some big houses that were grandly called villas they were not really so big when several servants were expected to live together under the same roof, but independently from the owners. The owners demanded privacy, desiring as little contact as possible with the servants, but this was difficult. The houses were not designed to house servants and not large enough to be adapted effectively. There was no second staircase – backstairs – for exclusive use by the staff, making it difficult to avoid the family. This was a major problem for Rebekah and, after her death, for me. There were also two male staff, Vern who looked after the horses and Stanley who drove the carriage, kept it clean and did the heavy chores around the house and tended the garden. They shared the living area over the stables but came into the kitchen to eat meals with us. Old Mrs Waters was present during these breaks, keeping an eye on us to make sure we behaved to her satisfaction.

Sister Kathleen interrupted, 'Why ever did you return to Towitta after you had escaped such a horrible place?'

'Be patient, Sister, and I'll tell you. Believe me it was not my choice.'

I was called home by Father at the time my mistress's husband, a well-known city businessman, started to become over-friendly with me. By this time I had become attached to his family, especially his little girl. I was happy. I was told he'd made a fortune from the goldfields in Western Australia and in the silver mines at Broken Hill; that their house was built from the profits using the finest materials and one of Adelaide's best architects.

Then Rebekah's troubles began, and I became involved too. Rebekah and I were very close and for the first year we shared a room. Then I was given the tiny boxroom as my own. Madam had decided I should have my own room until such time it could be used as a nursery, when I'd have to return to share a room with Rebekah. I didn't mind this. Rebekah and I would talk for ages before we went to sleep. She trained me in the running of the household, and told me of all the goings-on as she saw them.

Sweet Rebekah with her fair curly hair spoke from experience when she told me that the men who called themselves gentlemen and had important business positions about town, were not gentlemen at all. She constantly warned me to keep my door locked at night. I was puzzled. I couldn't think why she should insist on this in a house safe from intruders. It didn't occur to me she was referring to dangers from within the house. She believed all men were cads and bounders by nature, men who promised the world to prove their so-called sincerity, who gave trifling gifts and trinkets for 'little favours'.

I discovered she knew what she was talking about from experience, for one day she asked me to accompany her to a herbalist living on North Terrace who could help her out of her delicate condition. I was startled when she told me this for although we went out on the town together and often met young men of our own ages, we didn't have sweethearts. So I was baffled as to how she'd managed to get herself in the family way until I remembered her warnings about locking the bedroom door. Just before she died she whispered that the intruder was none other than our mistress's husband, and that I had better watch out.

On the morning of the visit, Rebekah told madam she was not feeling well and needed to see a doctor. In the afternoon she was given time off and I was asked to chaperone her. We went to the smart terrace houses next to the Botanic Hotel on North Terrace and I waited for her outside.

Sister Kathleen couldn't contain herself at this, 'My goodness, I remember now that some of the older nurses were talking about the terraces next to the Botanic Hotel and why they were so popular with country women travelling alone. They never explained how the boarding houses were connected to the hospital. They kept making references but, Mary, I've been so naïve!'

The trick was to start a miscarriage by visiting one of the 'herbalists' and then admit yourself to the hospital if things went wrong. About half an hour after Rebekah asked me to wait outside, she appeared looking pale. 'Now I shall be all right,' she said quietly.

'What have you done, Rebekah?' I asked. But by now I had guessed. Sometimes the servants about town talked of these occurrences. The next morning when I arose early, I found Rebekah slumped on the kitchen floor by the wood stove in a pool of blood. I ran and summoned Madam who immediately sent the carriage driver for a doctor and the police. Rebekah was rushed to hospital, where she died an agonising death from septicaemia many days later.

Before she died she told the police at her bedside that she had visited Madam Harpur for a certain operation. Madam Harpur called herself a herbalist and she was well known to the police for long-suspected illegal abortions. It was during this time that I first met Detective Bill Priest, the well-known Adelaide 'D', who came to interview us. Although Rebekah told me the man responsible for her condition, the police were unable to draw this information from her before she died.

'Now, Miss Schippan,' Detective Priest asked, 'are you sure Rebekah never told you who her sweetheart was?'

'No, sir, she never told me.'

Despite the probing questions, the detective was unable to obtain the information he was looking for, which he referred to as corroborative evidence. Madam Harpur was not convicted on this occasion.

Work in the big house did not stop but it continued in uncomfortable and miserable silence until the funeral. After the funeral I took over Rebekah's place in the household with the promise of extra help and moved back into the bigger room I had shared with her in those happy early days. It had become difficult to find girls who were happy and able to work as a domestic servant. Madam said so many girls were saucy and forward, and so several came and went. The stress of running the household on my own and dealing with the master played on my already delicate health, almost to the point of breaking down.

By this time, I knew my mistress was in the family way again because she was sick every morning. It was then that her husband began deliberately blocking my way on the stairs or in passageways. He would come up behind me when I was dusting or bending over and place his hands on me, oh, ever so gently. He always made it seem like an accident. He apologised and I couldn't take offence, especially as he was a gentleman and me a maid, and he knew when to give one of his smiles. It became a most difficult situation. Who could I tell, who would believe me, and further, was I imagining it? After a while I came to accept that he would never pass without a caress. And it was no surprise that these gentle collisions led to other kinds of encounters.

When his wife and small daughter went to stay with her sister in the country for a few weeks, the deaf old Mrs Waters remained in the house. But this did not deter the master who took to coming into my room each night after returning from his club, no matter how late or how much under the influence he was. The first time he came to me he made out that he'd entered my room by mistake.

'I'm so sorry, Miss Schippan, I didn't mean to wake you.'

'There is no need to apologise, sir.'

'Look, you have been here a long time now, may I call you Mary?' and he moved to sit on my bed and make himself comfortable. 'I've been meaning to tell you how impressed I am with you. Don't think I haven't noticed how you do your hair and wear your clothes. I see how neat and efficient you are. But you act as quiet and timid as a little mouse while watching me out of the corner of your eye. I notice these things. And of course, every time I pass you in the hall or on the stairs, you never fend me off. When I put my hands on you, you yearn for me, don't you? Don't say a word, Mary. I know what you want.'

By this time I am unable to speak or move. I am paralysed with disbelief and shock for he has moved closer and begun running his fingers gently over my neck and throat.

Sister Kathleen's eyes were wide when she asked, 'Why didn't you stop him there and then?'

'Don't you see, Sister, I couldn't – and more truthfully I didn't want to.'

Once he'd started caressing my throat and running his hands under my nightdress, I felt my whole body brace itself … waiting … waiting. When I didn't push him away, he put his lips to my neck and … Well, if you must know, I was already his. I desired whatever he offered. So you see his gentle way of approaching me after he first came into my room, lead to other visits. And despite Rebekah's dire warning, I never learnt to lock my door. After my master's first visit, to start locking it would have been useless. I wanted him and besides, locking the door would not have stopped him as he had spare keys. And I believed that if I refused him he would find reason to have me sacked. I could not risk forgoing a reference. The alternative was to return to Towitta. As well as knowing Rebekah's fate, I'd heard about seduced servants resorting to dumping newborn infants on the doorsteps of strangers, down privies or into the Torrens Lake. Worse still, single mothers-to-be could end up at female refuges or at the government's prison-like lying-in department at the destitute asylum.

After his wife returned from her vacation, George – that is Mr Waters – continued visiting me until after her confinement.

I liked these nightly visits. In the mornings when I woke I sometimes found a bottle of scent or a lacy handkerchief on my dressing table. But I was scared of the consequences and knew I had to leave as soon as I found another position – or before I was sacked.

The worry of being put in the family way and disgraced, or ending up like Rebekah, exacerbated my illness. During this time I was suddenly taken ill, the haemorrhage making me believe I might have been in a delicate condition myself. Later I fainted. Madam insisted a doctor be called in to attend to me. I wasn't keen to see one, hoping it was all due to the nights of interrupted sleep, but believing it to be something worse …

It turned out she was right in sending for a doctor as I was diagnosed with the early stages of consumption, the same disease that had afflicted my sister Pauline for two years before her death. I don't know why Pauline and I suffered, no one else in the family had it. Although Madam advised me to return to my parents as soon as possible, I was kept on until a new servant could be found. The doctor advised that the new health nurse from the City Council would visit me and speak with Madam. She told Madam that although I was not infectious she would leave a list of health instructions that we had to follow. I could see Madam was unhappy about the nurse's opinion. The nurse convinced me that I should return immediately to the country, to the fresh air and all the benefits that rural life would give me. Madam and I were unsure as to what to do for the best.

I knew I had to leave but I dreaded returning to Towitta. I was in a dilemma. Madam felt I should return to my parents but she didn't want to lose me as I would be hard to replace. I thought of finding another situation with the reference she'd provided, intended for when I was well again. I thought I would have no difficulty in securing another situation. Madam told me that but for the tuberculosis, I could have had a job with her for as long as I liked. In the meantime I thought of other possibilities as I carried on with my job.

If Madam told her husband of my condition it didn't change his ways; his visits continued for a few more weeks. They only stopped when Dora, the nurse for the new baby, was taken on. It meant that she had to move in and share the room with me for the baby now slept in the former boxroom. It was a blessed relief in many ways but secretly I missed those nightly visits. Perhaps it explained why I became moody and difficult at times. I squabbled with Dora and the stablehands and snapped at Mrs Waters.

Only a few weeks later, when I was still trying to find another situation without upsetting Madam, Father wrote to Mr Waters telling him I was needed urgently at home. My sister Pauline, who had suffered from tuberculosis for some time, had taken a turn for the worse and was given only a matter of weeks to live. I was in a panic. I could not imagine life at home without her. My older sister was the only loving person in our family. And now I had been diagnosed with the disease too. What would happen to me? Would I also die?

Madam had not found a servant to replace me by the time I left the household. I felt guilty at leaving her with so much work to do in the house. She decided to look after the baby herself, while the baby's nurse agreed to do my work for a short time for an increase in her wages. Madam was very kind to me but there was some relief in leaving that situation because I was worried to death about becoming pregnant – although I can't say I was pleased at leaving Adelaide and giving up the independence I had gained. It was painful leaving that household, leaving a mistress who was kind and considerate. Far worse though, was leaving her husband, George, who taught me how less frightening the nights could be, even enjoyable when there was someone special to share them with. It was with much reluctance that I returned to Towitta.

Sister Kathleen was shaking her head with disbelief, not only about my amorous time with Mr Waters.

'How dreadful that you had to return. I know you had no option with your sister being ill, but I think I would have gone mad at the thought, or drowned myself in the Torrens Lake.'

'If I hadn't gone back, believe me my father would have come to fetch me. Had I found somewhere to hide for a time, he would have called in the police to find me. There was no escape. Father could have had me incarcerated into a lunatic asylum for my own protection. I took liberties, but where has it got me? For our sins, the evil eye gets us all in the end.'

## 10

Mother and my sisters were glad to have me home. But going home made no difference to brothers Willy and August. They were very poor company anyway, except for each other. They went about their chores quietly enough, minding the sheep and mending the fences for Father. Every few days they'd go off into the bush, into the distant hills or up the Cowlands or Towitta creeks and shoot galahs, rabbits, and the occasional kangaroo or emu. These hunts never included Bertha or me of course. We never wanted to go anyway. Bertha relied on Mother and me when she couldn't play with the Matschoss girls.

Some people called my younger brothers backward. But they weren't, they were just a bit slower, different to other boys. When people saw Willy's stooped frame, his pigeon chest and scissor-type legs for the first time it made them feel uncomfortable. Mother thought this misshaped body was associated with the fits he had from time to time that usually followed bouts of breathlessness. She called it his nerves because he became distressed when there was unpleasantness brought about by Father. Little children were known to scream with fright when they saw Willy for he looked like he'd jumped out of the pages of a Wendish folktale. August's slow and quiet manner fooled most, but he was not dumb. People just treated him like Willy because they were always together.

The boys never laughed, sang or even talked much that anyone noticed. They avoided contact with others and were deathly quiet, but they understood each other perfectly well with the sign language that included the merest of body movements and eye contact. They would slink away unnoticed in the same way they sometimes appeared, almost from nowhere. Once Father's chores were done, they vanished into the bush until mealtimes or bedtime. They had their own guns and when they had a supply of bullets they shot anything on sight that would make a stew or decorate their hats or clothes.

In the springtime, when the sun's gentle warmth could turn to blazing heat, snakes slithered into shady spots around the house and it became a haven for the several varieties. My sisters and I were scared of these creatures for they were often more than five feet long with venomous bites that could kill. If none of the men were around to blast them with a shotgun, one of us girls dashed for a gun and shot them ourselves. Those not shot often slithered inside and simply disappeared, only to be found coiled up in a pile of laundry hours later. More frightening was when we found one in the bedroom.

August and Willy loved nothing better than being brave and protecting us by blasting them to pieces. 'Show me where it is and stand back,' August would say after retrieving the shotgun from Father's gun cupboard. The walls of the house were decorated by bullet holes until the yearly whitewashing when they were filled in again.

Willy and August were not at all like their older brothers who were normal in every way. Noisy and mischievous, Frederick and Heinrich battled with Father every day, unlike the younger brothers who were deathly quiet and terrified of Father. They got their revenge on the world by frightening Bertha with their gory attention to cutting up the creatures they killed and chasing after her with bloodied limbs or entrails, laughing and hooting with the sheer delight of seeing her running away from them in terror. These were the only times I saw them truly happy. This love of killing wild creatures and hanging up entrails had convinced the locals that there was something disturbingly odd about them. They were convinced that these habits would surely lead August and Willy to killing people. When anyone visited the farmhouse the brothers would vanish.

Although the boys went to the one-roomed school in the only street of Towitta and learnt English, we spoke to them in a combination of Wendish and German. Perhaps in doing so we weren't helping them very much to make their way in the world of English speakers. They spoke English with a thick guttural accent and non-Germans found it difficult to understand them at all.

## 11

I remembered how numbing it was to have to return to Father's household, losing my freedom even though I had just had my twenty-second birthday. It meant giving up a regular wage with food and board and most of Sunday free. Now Mother could care for Pauline while I did more of the farm chores. Back at the farm in the wilderness I despaired at how much I missed the hustle and bustle of Adelaide. I wondered if I would go mad. Father imposed his restrictions as before, making life cramped and unbearable. I was treated like my sister Bertha. I was humiliated by the lack of regard given for my age or the independence I had enjoyed in Adelaide.

'You're not in Adelaide now,' Father shouted. 'I'll have no daughter of mine bringing her fancy city ideas here and shaming me in front of our neighbours. While you're under my roof you'll do as I say. Is that clear?' And I lost my temper frequently in return, which did no good as I was punished with a leather strap or locked up. One night I was whipped after taking food to the barn to Willy and August, denied supper for being late home from hunting. Then as if this wasn't enough, I was locked in the smaller timber barn that creaked and groaned like witches even when there was hardly a breath of wind. So I learned to remain quiet and demure, while inside I raged and my thoughts were as black as a moonless night.

On my return home I witnessed Pauline's grave condition. Pauline was close to Mother, her imminent death made Mother weepy and prone to collapsing with grief. It was when Mother's sorrow made her unable to keep up with the chores that Mathes wrote to Mrs Waters requesting my return. I arrived home six weeks before Christmas, a frantic time for Wendish and German women. Although Bertha undertook the daily chores of feeding the animals and sweeping out the house, Mother wanted me to do the extra baking, the general cooking and the preparations that came with the season. We prepared slabs of German cake known as *Streuselküchen* ideal for large gatherings of relatives at Christmas time. We baked honey cakes called *Honigküchen* which we cut into shapes and hung on the Christmas tree, in our case a small native pine. Christmas was usually one of the more happy events of the year when even Father was known to sing a rousing carol. This year, any merriment there could have been, was marred by Pauline's perilous condition.

Doctor Pullen made several visits and told Mother that Pauline was already too ill to make the journey to the Consumptive Home in Adelaide. 'I'm afraid there's nothing more I can do for her. It could be any day now. Just keep her as comfortable as possible. She may die in her sleep, the best outcome for all, but I fear she'll have an attack before that happens. It will be painful watching her struggle for breath. I hope her demise will be quick and peaceful. This will not make for a merry Christmas, all your festive preparations will be for a funeral instead.'

When I returned from Adelaide, Bertha was moved back into Mother's room to sleep on a stretcher bed. I slept in the iron bed with Pauline. Each night as I held her I wondered if it would be her last. She often cried in my arms saying how different things would have been if Mr Khan had been alive and how fleeing from Towitta would have changed her life for the better. I usually sobbed in agreement, seeing now what my own plight was likely to be. I didn't stop her saying all these things for I knew it was fantasy. 'Mary, I'm not crying because I'm dying. I'm more than glad to leave this cruel and sinful world. I cry for what might have been with Mr Khan and me. When you're feeling strong enough go as far away as possible. Heed my words, no good will come of you staying in this godforsaken place.'

Of course what she said was true. I didn't want to end up

like her, unmarried and infected with the same disease. 'I can't bear to lose you but I will not die like you, please don't say that I will. I feel well, just a little weary. No more talk of dying now. Who will I share my secrets with after you've gone? Bertha's not like us, and she's too young to understand the kind of things you and I talk about.'

The nights leading to Pauline's death became unsettled with her increased coughing. Each night before I joined her in bed, I put a bowl of water and some clean rags on the chest of drawers in preparation. She'd fall asleep without fuss but then wake in the night having a fit which seemed to be brought on when she stopped breathing. It was agonising listening to her desperate attempts to gain air. The rasping, wheezing and choking sounds kept us awake and I had to clean her up. I was allowed a lamp during this time and I would climb out of bed and light it when Pauline had these distressing turns. I wiped her face and handed her a rag to cough into. As she heaved and spluttered fighting for air, the bed linen became soiled and it became a daily ritual for me to boil out the stains in the copper. This only set of linen dried quickly in the hot, dry summer air.

None of the family in the house slept well during Pauline's last days. On her final night Father and Mother were woken by the desperate sounds of her struggling for breath, and they came to our room with Bertha. They suspected death was close. Mother and I sat either side of Pauline murmuring words of comfort and wiping her as the sweat poured off her. Bertha cried and Father merely sat at the back of the room with the lamp and his Bible and read aloud passages and psalms in the form of last rites. His reading from the Bible did not provide comfort for me.

The struggle ended when Pauline had a violent coughing fit which left her too weak to breathe. She looked more peaceful than I had seen her since my return home. Father and Bertha returned to bed. Mother and I quickly set to and laid her out, pausing to cry in each other's arms. This was the only time

I could remember being truly comforted by Mother. Mother didn't feel it was proper for me to climb back into bed with a dead sister, as much as I longed to hold her. I was such a nervy person that I would rarely venture outdoors at night, not even to one of the barns. But that night I had no choice and went and found a place in the barn. August and Willy didn't stir when I joined them for the night.

Nothing disturbed the boys once they had gone to sleep, not even a storm or the dog barking. So it was my lot to wake them early in the morning and tell them Pauline had died in the night. I had never seen the brothers cry and when I told them about Pauline's death they did not seem to understand at first. They looked at me stunned. Then August said to Willy, 'Like the birds, Willy, when they have gone to sleep.'

Willy replied, 'But she is asleep, isn't she? She will wake up soon, won't she, our Mary?'

'No, Willy,' explained August. 'Pauline's gone for good and we will have to bury her in a deep hole at the Sedan cemetery. Because that's what happens when people go to sleep forever.'

At last Willy understood and began an outpouring of wailing and sobbing that took some time for August and me to quell. It was our grief too; the tears were streaming down our faces. We finally composed ourselves before dressing and heading for the kitchen. As soon as breakfast was over August was sent away in the wagon to fetch the undertaker from Sedan.

## 12

Pauline was their angel. When she died there was no one left to nurture August and Willy in her gentle caring way. Father called her 'God's little helper'. It was as though she was made from the caring parts missing from our Mother. Pauline treated the boys how they thought a true mother should. She was kind and held them in her arms when they were frightened or when they had been punished by Father or scolded by Mother. It was Pauline who tended their grazed knees, took out the splinters, combed their hair and scrubbed them clean in the tin bath when they were younger.

Mother merely treated them as two more of the farm animals that regularly needed feeding, and left them in Pauline's charge. I helped Pauline but I wasn't like her. I was often lost in my thoughts. August could be talking to me for some time before he realised I hadn't heard a word. I told them I could slip away from Father by just going into a daze. Well according to them, I was in a daze most of the time. They never really knew where they stood with me, one minute I would go behind Father's back and bring them dinner when Father had punished them, and then suddenly I would start screaming and shouting about something they'd done. That's just how it was. I was not calm and collected like Pauline.

August and Willy knew Pauline was going to die. After the doctor visited one day when she couldn't get out of bed or stop coughing and wheezing, she told them so. At first they were very upset because they thought it was going to happen in the next few hours, but she didn't die for ages. Her illness dragged on, and every morning they sighed with relief when they came into the kitchen for breakfast and saw her standing there ladling out porridge or cutting up the bread. She always greeted them in a way that told them she was glad to see them.

The days were bearable while Pauline was there. One morning she wasn't in the kitchen for breakfast, she had become too weak to climb out of bed. And there she stayed. When she did die, the light went out of their lives. August was seventeen and Willy fifteen.

Willy thought he knew about death. When he shot a galah or a possum, it simply stopped in its tracks and went limp. Bright and glinty eyes glazed over and when he held a creature in his hands to take a closer look, its head hung down and swung freely. As much as he poked them after they were shot or trapped, they would not wake up from this sleep. This is how Pauline appeared to him when she died, just asleep. He poked her and pleaded with her to talk to them but I said she'd gone and that he mustn't touch her again or try and wake her. She had gone to sleep forever. Yet, if it was just sleep, why couldn't he wake her?

Willy and August were pleased they slept in a barn, like most farm boys their age, especially on the night following Pauline's death. August told me much later that when he and Willy went to sleep in the barn that night, they both wept into their straw mattresses not caring that they could hear each other crying like babies and spurring each other on into louder wails of grief and sobbing. Father always said that boys don't cry, but they did that night and they didn't care who heard them. After that they didn't cry again, not even when Bertha was slain by the strange intruder.

The boys wanted to discover where a creature went when it died, so they cut them up to try and catch them at the moment when they left the body. Soon after the creatures died, parts of them twitched or throbbed, which baffled the boys. They fell into the habit of cutting up animals they killed and taking out their entrails, at first to inspect them but then because it gave them something to do. When they became more confident of what they were doing, they ran around with bloodied entrails to frighten Bertha.

There were other aspects of death that neither of them could understand. Mother and Father confused them when talking of Heaven, telling the boys that creatures didn't go to Heaven like Pauline had because they had no soul. This was a puzzle. Then Mother and Father told them of the hideous place where bad people went. A place named Hell. So August and Willy spent a lot of time wondering which members in the family would go to Hell. I told them, 'You two will go there if you don't stop killing innocent creatures.' But then I confused them further by telling them they need not fear going to Hell because they were already living in it with Father.

August knew he and Willy weren't like their older brothers Frederick and Heinrich. When they had been around, life wasn't quite so bad for August and Willy because Father left them alone while he bullied the older boys. And before the two eldest ran away the four boys had enjoyed good times together. They had teased August and Willy all the time, but in fun. How the younger boys missed their brothers! They showed them how to hunt and kill, to fence, chop wood, and most of all how to keep out of the way of bad-tempered people. Our family was made up of bad moods or cold silences. Horrid things happened in our family. When August and Willy were much older and their big brothers were settled at a cattle station in the far north of South Australia, they returned to rescue them, taking them away on a train to some place in the desert. Later, all the brothers changed their names and spent much of their adult lives in the saddle where they were able to forget their unhappy childhoods at Towitta. Who could blame them?

Bertha seemed to cause trouble just by being around. She was spirited, and oh so boisterous – cheeky too. She simply got on my nerves. Yet whereas August was clobbered for insolence, as Father called it, she escaped punishment for far more serious acts of disobedience. Pauline seemed able to calm Bertha, August and Willy too, but I seemed to seethe all the time. At times when they talked to me I'd be far away lost in my own thoughts. I laughed a lot when Pauline was alive, but that stopped when she died. Pauline and I had been as thick as thieves, as were Willy and August, and Frederick and Heinrich. But Bertha was on her own.

After Pauline died the house fell into a stony silence except when someone was losing their temper, which seemed to be a daily occurrence. Bertha tried to move into the space near me made empty by Pauline's death, but I kept the precocious child at a distance. Bertha thought if she followed me around I'd give in to her. She seemed to want to get inside my thoughts all the time.

I was the most nervous, even more so than Willy. I was prone to nightmares and sleepwalking. It took a lot of noise to wake Willy and August in the barn, but even they were woken at times by my blood-curdling screams and clung to each other for safety. My nightmares were so frightening that in the hour before bed I paced the floor anxiously. At times Mother and Father would try to calm me down, sometimes by shouting at me, 'Oh for goodness sake, girl, settle down. Read from the good book and take comfort from it.'

Mother made me sleeping draughts from her herbal brews during the worse times, but they only made my dreams more vivid. When my sleepwalking was at its worst, Father locked me in the shed for my own safety. I told them the shed breathed like it was alive and full of witches. So although I was pre-vented from wandering off, August and Willy had to put up with my mournful wailing and sobbing in terror. They sympa-thised with me because they often frightened each other with those terrifying stories August read from the green book that belonged to Father. They knew what it was to be frightened of the dark.

Mind you, they loved to hear me telling the fairytales that sprang from my vivid imagination. August thought I not only frightened them to death but probably myself. I relished tales of child-killing monsters and witches that grabbed you in the scrub. When the boys thought they heard mysterious noises in the bush, they became riveted with fear. Other times they simply ran for their lives.

Why would they doubt me? I told even better stories than Father. But Father said my brand of storytelling would get me into trouble one day, I distorted the truth and took things to extremes. And then the storytelling stopped, I became too sick and had times when I was bed-bound. The boys learned I had the same sickness as Pauline and that I too could die from it, but I knew they wouldn't cry for me when I died.

Having lost Pauline Mother insisted she wasn't going to lose me. She believed I could be cured from consumption by certain concoctions she'd heard about. She wrote to an Adelaide Chinese herbalist named Lum Yow. Some people believed him a Chinese quack. She sent for a recipe and everyday a mixture of turpentine and oil or turpentine and butter was rubbed over my body. It was a revolting smelly mixture and as much as I protested, Mother made sure I rubbed it in well.

There was another cure-all she made, a kind of pickle of brandy and salt. When Mother insisted on making this brew, Father, who never touched a drop of alcohol, was unhappy about going to the hotel in Sedan to buy a bottle of brandy. But Mother put on a turn about losing another of her daughters to the 'white plague' if he didn't. After her pleas and tears, he drove the buggy to Sedan and stony-faced bought a bottle of the 'demon drink'. I often wondered what the folks at the bar thought when my father entered to buy a bottle, but apparently the Meyers didn't bat an eyelid. Mother made me take a table-spoon of this mixture, two or three times a week. A few weeks later, when my health seemed to have improved, she insisted her remedies had worked.

'I swear, Mary, there is a bloom in your cheeks and you have your appetite back.'

'If you say so, Mother.'

Father responded to my improved health by reminding me of the sin he had committed in going to the pub on my behalf. His pride and dignity were sorely tested and I had to suffer because of it.

While I could escape into my fantasies or retreat to the peace by one of the creeks, it was a strain when darkness fell and we were shut up in the house together. I guess Mother could no longer stand the tension and misery either, I know I could hardly bear it, so she came to my rescue by securing me a job through her friends in Angaston. She thought it would help me recover from Pauline's death, but more importantly she wanted me out of Father's hair as it would calm both our tempers.

While I had been working in Adelaide, Father had begun building a bigger farmhouse with the extra money I sent home each week. When I returned home he could no longer pay for the materials needed to finish it. This frustrated him and I was blamed. Starting work at the Yalumba Fruit Preserve factory meant that Father could finish the half-built structure. I was angry to think that part of my precious hard-earned wage was going toward this when it could have been used by Mother to decorate and furnish the existing house.

It was in the weeks before I left Towitta to work in Adelaide that my two eldest brothers, Frederick and Heinrich, went to live with our Aunt Giscelia, Father's sister, in Eden Valley. Mother had come to their rescue, this time claiming that the farm could no longer support them because of the worsening drought conditions, but it was really because of the one and only whipping they had given Father before fleeing.

Mother was distraught but somehow she had enough gumption to defy Father for she took the buggy and drove to Eden Valley to see Aunt Giscelia to secure a safe refuge for Frederick and Heinrich. She was gone a night and a day and two days after she returned, the two eldest brothers went to live there. Later, they travelled to the far north of South Australia to work on a cattle station. Frederick came back for Bertha's funeral and later made the journey to Adelaide for my court trial.

## 13

With the older boys and Pauline gone from the farm, there were just four of us children left at home with Mother and Father. Bertha was the youngest at thirteen years. Willy and August had taken over the farm work from the older brothers. Although life at home was at first more peaceful, the two younger brothers now attracted more attention from Father than before. I suppose it was nothing less than bullying. They couldn't help being how they were, slower than the older brothers at completing chores. Father continually ordered them to hurry. He'd bawl, 'Get a move on, you potato heads. I want that hay cut today not next week.'

The boys cowered, fearing Father and his whip, but they were not fast enough to jump out of the way of its stinging lashes as Frederick and Heinrich had been. Although there were now three less mouths to feed, our family of six struggled to survive on a farm that could barely feed one.

Despite Father's outburst, when he learned I had taken the job in Angaston he simmered down and allowed me to go. Boarding there with old friends of Mother's in the week, I travelled home every fortnight or so for the weekend. I hated going home, but I was expected to bring back my wages to help keep the farm going. My life in Angaston was calm and peaceful, and it was a trial to make the regular journeys to Towitta. During a school holiday in the late autumn, a busy period at the factory, Bertha joined me. The factory manager had approached Father on one of his rare visits to Angaston.

Bertha was well developed and, for one so young, what some would consider forward. She was taller than me and stronger. When the dust was at its worst and invaded our hair, her auburn mane seemed to increase in size resembling a huge boxthorn hedge. It made her look even bigger, older and quite wild.

Father always said she was the one who looked most like his father. She looked far older than her years and loved the attention men of all ages gave her, the young daring men openly flirting with her. Who could blame them, she was striking.

This situation caused me much stress for I was threatened with recall if I couldn't chaperone Bertha at all times and keep her safe. When gossip from a well-meaning friend reached Father about her flirtations, he threatened to bring us home and thrash me for bringing shame on our family. When Mother's friend warned Bertha our father knew about her behaviour and about the likely repercussions, Bertha hurriedly sent Father a note to pacify him. Unlike me she knew how to get round him; my brothers and I never had a chance.

At the Angaston fruit factory I shared my dinner breaks under the trees or a verandah with a small group of unmarried women. Like other factories that employ so many we soon divided into groups. Few of the young women in my group had ever been to Adelaide, so they enjoyed the stories of my adventures. They wanted to know about the family I worked for, a family they had heard about or read about in the social pages of the newspapers. What I wanted more than anything was to share with them stories of the passionate nights I spent with my master, how he held me in his arms and stroked me. But, of course, I did not.

I told them instead about the master's flirting, about him trapping us on the stairs and in the corridors. It's what they expected. They'd heard about this happening to many girls who had gone to work in Adelaide. And so when I told them such things had happened to me, that he caressed my back as I swept the stairs, the girls would clamour, 'What did you do about it?'

The girls' imaginations were stirred up by my stories; they agreed I was the best storyteller they'd known. I remembered Father's words and told my listeners, 'The tales are always true and you'd better believe them.'

My new friends wanted more stories. So at night I would think up a new story for the next day about my life in Adelaide. As you can appreciate, I added details that made even everyday chores sound exciting. Although they were never sure where fiction took over from fact, they were starved of tales about Adelaide and happy to imagine my life in a bustling sinful city. They couldn't understand what I was doing in Angaston.

'Wouldn't you rather be in Adelaide?' they asked.

'Of course I would.'

I told them that when I was better I expected to return to Adelaide to find another position. Secretly, although I longed to escape there, I knew this was unlikely.

# 14

'Tell me of your sweetheart, Mary. How did you meet him? From the photographs in old newspapers at home, I remember him as handsome.'

Sister Kathleen was keen to know where Gustave came into the story. I had been determined to tell as much as possible of my life story before he appeared. But now the time had come for me to talk of him.

Well, he was bronzed by the sun and wind and I thought him handsome. I met him while travelling to and from Angaston, up and down Parrot or Accommodation Hill. He was a year younger than me. Bertha had finished her few weeks at the factory, and I was relieved. On the weekend I accompanied her back to Towitta, I remember Gustave showing off to her. He performed tricks with the horses, and told her of his exploits in Adelaide. Of course she listened intently, smiling and catching his eye.

Gustave Nitschke was a delivery boy who worked for the Schwanefeldts. They were local traders in Sedan with business premises in Adelaide. He would do the rounds of nearby towns and travel to Adelaide about once a fortnight, staying overnight in Carrington Street with relatives of his employer. I often rode home with him when he was going to Sedan. He would turn off the main road and drop me close to the farm before heading through Towitta back onto the main road. Often there were other passengers who paid a shilling or two for the lift.

These journeys took several hours so it was a pleasant opportunity to talk with people one wouldn't otherwise have the chance to speak with. I admired the way Gustave handled the six spirited chestnut and bay horses as I sat up beside him and looked along their sweating backs. He handled them with no harshness or cruelty, with hardly a touch of a whip. When he stopped to give them a rest they looked for his soothing words, titbits and the stroking of their heads. I think it was his kindness and genuine affection for these powerful but gentle creatures that first attracted me to him.

For several journeys we didn't speak, then one day he asked me, 'Miss Schippan, has the cat stolen your tongue?'

'Not at all, Mr Nitschke. I barely know you.'

'Well you should by now. We've travelled together several times, hours spent without a word. You can't sit there in silence any longer. It's quite nerve racking, you know.'

This broke the silence and we began to exchange niceties. I considered him brazen, but I couldn't resist being friendly. He was a sunny kind of person and it wasn't long before we were drawn to each other. It was a long journey after all, and it was difficult to meet suitable young men in such an isolated place.

I liked it best when Gustave and I travelled alone. When the weather was fair and there was just us, he would stop at the top of the treacherous hill with miles of stone walls before the long descent to Towitta and Sedan. He'd tether the horses and we'd go and sit behind a stone wall and gaze at the countryside spread out far below us like a patchwork quilt; different hues of brown or gold in summer and greens and smoky blues in the winter. There was nothing remarkable in the landscape other than the changing colours, and because nothing stood out on the river flats that could create a relief in the landscape, not a shadow fell.

It was on one of these picnics hidden in the long grass in perfect weather that we became lovers. In the winter wind and rain the journey could be treacherous and miserable despite the canvas hood erected for such weather. No matter how bad the weather was, if we were alone we stopped somewhere for an hour or sometimes more. In the covered wagon we made a warm cosy love nest despite the wind howling overhead or a rare downpour of rain.

I was impatient for these breaks when we could be together, looking down onto the flats. We would eat our picnic of fresh crusty bread, cheese and pickled dill cucumbers on an old tarpaulin. The times when we were alone together were rare but we knew how to share in the passion we had found.

Towards the end of the year we were officially a courting couple and Gustave and I made plans for leaving the Murray Plains for good before the heat of summer arrived. He heard about a job that would soon be vacant as a driver for one of the many carrier companies in the city. I had Mrs Waters' reference to help me find another servant's position in the city. We would be able to save enough money to settle down and have our own family. I was over the age of consent and not even Father could stop me. Yet he tried, saying how much Mother relied on me at weekends. He knew how to generate guilt.

On one of these stops I was lying on the tarpaulin. Gustave stood in front of me in rolled-up shirtsleeves with an open neck and a long juicy grass stem in his mouth. 'What about if we leave here and go to Adelaide at the end of November before it gets too hot,' he suggested. 'I already have enough money saved for when we live there. I have been saving for years, you know.'

Surprised and pleased I replied, 'What are you suggesting Gustave Nitschke? Are you intending to make an honest woman of me then?'

'If you like. We'll find work in Adelaide and wait until our families have forgiven us for running away. They'll want to arrange a proper wedding with all the fuss and bother that entails. They won't take kindly to us running off to Adelaide, you know. Your Father will accuse us of dishonouring and shaming the family and his church and may want us expelled from the congregation. Do you think you can cope with that?' he asked gently. 'You realise our churches may not allow us back there to be married if we leave our families. And arranging a wedding to suit the two different strands of the Lutheran Church would bring too much bad blood into our families.'

'When I leave here, I don't care what the church thinks. Anyway, Father keeps reminding us that he can't afford to pay for a wedding for any of us, no matter how humble. Couldn't we have one of those civil weddings or something, or even get married in one of the Lutheran churches in the city? I don't really care how we do it or which branch we choose so long as we leave here. And when I do, I'm never coming back.'

'You sound harsh.'

'You have no idea what it's been like to live out here in the middle of nowhere with Father, and nothing to look forward to. Don't you see, I'm at my wit's end. I'm twenty-four now and Father still beats me and chastises me for all my imperfections. Have you any idea of the humiliation?' Gustave couldn't answer that question.

But once we had decided to leave Towitta, nothing further happened. He wouldn't discuss it and I didn't know why. His silence began to wear heavily on my nerves; what had happened to the urgency? Spring was quickly moving towards summer.

These trips to and from Angaston each fortnight had been a highlight which I eagerly anticipated. Maybe because of the strain of our stalled courtship plans, I began having fits again and fainting more often. When the doctor examined me and declared me unfit for work until my health improved, I grudgingly returned to Towitta and my total dependence on Father, having to beg for every item I needed.

There was no doubt that Mother was glad to have me back home, for apart from Bertha and those visiting commercial travellers and hawkers prepared to put up with Father's insults, I was all the company she had. Although our nearest neighbours were less than a quarter of a mile away, sometimes we didn't see anyone for days. When my health rallied I did most of the housework, and also helped with the farm work now that the older brothers had left home and Pauline had died. I was nothing more than an unpaid drudge.

There was always much to do and in my melancholy state,

even though Gustave paid me visits, I gradually paid less attention to my appearance. My hair was unkempt. I wore the same clothes for days at a time. Apart from clothes that were worn for best, such as on Sunday when we went to church, I had only one dress and a skirt. I was moody and raging with anger, tightly coiled like a spring ready to be released at a touch. Even Gustave's visits did little to comfort me. Even though he was cheerful, cocky and cheeky I was beginning to doubt him. He never made deliveries to us, but he would make a diversion from the main Towitta track to the farm. He saw me at my worst. My clothes were usually splattered with sheep or pig's blood, and I was often too busy to stop although weary and bored by the same routine, day in and day out. It was at this time of the year, after the crop of new sheep and pigs were born, that Father ordered us to slaughter the older stock. We smoked the meat and made sausages for Christmas, as well as preparing carcasses for sale to neighbours or Towitta villagers. That year the sale of the meat made little difference to the farm finances because of the mounting debts.

Yet my splattered dusty state and lack of interest only seemed to heighten Gustave's desire for me. He sometimes came back in the late afternoon or at the weekends to spend time with us. Sometimes I would trek over to the shady Cowlands Creek or to Towitta Creek and meet him there, far away from Father and Bertha's prying eyes. She liked his visits a little too much I thought. And he stirred her up with promises of visits to Sedan and even to Adelaide. I was not pleased at this form of flirtation with my not-so-little sister who took him at his word.

My parents did not stop his visits but they didn't exactly welcome him warmly. Father's remarks to Gustave were often gruff. I was in my twenties and my prospects of marriage depended heavily on him, yet this grudging acceptance of Gustave, if that's what it was, worried me. I couldn't work out what Father felt about having another man in his territory for he said nothing to me. But he behaved like a jealous lover, handling objects roughly, slamming doors shut and making rude remarks about his daughters being wayward, uncontrollable and the talk of the neighbourhood. Surely he objected to more then the fact we belonged to branches of the church that had been feuding?

As I said, although Gustave had always been affectionate, our relationship changed dramatically after I left the Angaston fruit factory. He refused to talk about us going to Adelaide and I became moody and sullen. One afternoon beside the nearby creek I asked Gustave, 'Are we still going to Adelaide?'.

'Of course, Mary.'

'But when?'

'I don't know, I have things to do first, things I cannot hurry.'

'But you have to,' I pleaded. 'If I stay here much longer I'll go crazy. Father is making my life Hell. Please can we settle on a date?'

'I'll see what I can do, Mary,' he said, avoiding eye contact.

'You promised weeks ago, don't you remember? But now there's something the matter, you don't seem so happy to be with me any more. You only come for one thing these days.'

'Now that's not fair, Mary. I have a lot on my mind, please don't push me.'

'But I have a lot to think about too,' I wailed. 'Father never lets me forget that as I no longer bring money into the household, I'm not worth anything, just another mouth to feed. Never mind that I work from morning to night for Mother and around the farm for him.'

'Look, I've told you I have to work something out. So for now I can't think about leaving here, until at least February.'

I was horrified. I felt betrayed. I couldn't believe that I had to put up with Towitta for at least three more months throughout the hottest and most unbearable months of the year – and with Father. 'You can't do this to me. You don't love me now that you've had your way with me.'

I demanded he tell me the reason he'd changed his plans. He refused to answer. In my frustration and anger I rushed at him and beat my clenched fists on his chest, crying with rage. He grabbed hold of my wrists and looked straight into my eyes and said firmly, 'That's how it is, Mary. I'm in a fix which I have to sort out. I can say no more.'

He pushed me aside and marched over to the horses standing quietly in the shade of the giant red gums along the creek. I was worried about losing him. Could I wait another three months? If he left that day with us fighting, I worried that he would not return. I swallowed my pride and asked him to return over the Christmas holiday period when my parents were away for several days. Things were a little merrier on his return, some of the passion was rekindled and we made new plans. I believed everything was going to be all right when he left me for a few days in Adelaide.

'Look, Sister, I don't want to talk about him any more today. It upsets me. I had blocked him from my mind and I didn't know he could still affect me so. We had plans for a happy future together in Adelaide, but after he left me that day, I never spoke with him again.' Sister Kathleen put her hand on my arm. 'Mary, I quite understand.'

'I don't believe you do, Sister, because I said goodbye to Gustave when he left for Adelaide, and the very next night Bertha was slain.'

'That is simply dreadful. Please don't say anything more now, you look white as a sheet.'

'I'll be all right, Sister, really I will. All this was so long ago now.'

'That may be so, but I don't think I can bear to hear any more today. Let me make you comfortable before I go.'

## 15

When Sister Kathleen looked in the next day, I was resting after a night of tears and anguish brought on by mentioning Gustave and feeling the pain of his loss.

'How are you feeling today, Mary?' Sister asked, always solicitous. I shrugged. I'm sure I looked tired and wretched.

'Perhaps we can sit on the verandah,' I suggested, 'and talk a little of other things. Tell me about your father who is a publican, and more of your German family.'

'Hmm. My Aunt Vera married into a medical family. They're quite well known – they had something to do with setting up a special German hospital. You may know it.'

'I do, everyone does, it's the one near Light's Pass, isn't it?'

'That's the one.'

'That's been there for decades. They mend bones and practise a special medicine, I believe. There's a name for it ... some kind of healing.'

'Yes, it's known as homeopathy. But enough about me today. Are you feeling strong enough to continue your story?'

'I'm strong enough, Sister,' I reassured her, 'but this might be a little hard for me. Until recently I had thought many times about Gustave and me all those years ago, and cried when I realised what I had lost. But until yesterday I had not talked about him to anyone.'

We dragged cane chairs to the verandah and Sister Kathleen left me to find refreshments. When she returned she handed me cake and prompted, 'What are you going to tell me today? Yesterday you stopped after Gustave went away. You mentioned Bertha's death.'

Oh yes, I remember. Well you can imagine my ordeal following that dreadful night when Bertha was killed. Our isolated farm was suddenly crawling with police and journalists. And, of course, those who lived in the area took a diversion past our gate to see what was happening at the Schippan farm. On the morning following Bertha's death, a Corporal Rumball and Dr Steel arrived at our farmhouse. A posse of police from Adelaide led by Detective Priest was not expected to arrive until the next day. When the detective's name was mentioned, I knew we had met before in Adelaide when Rebekah had died.

Our farm was filled with men with duties following a suspicious death. Soon after the arrival of Detective Priest and his men, these men stomped around with tape measures, notepads and pencils, spades and trowels. There were detectives, troopers on horses, trackers and messengers, as well as journalists from the Adelaide newspapers. I was told that these men were billeted around the neighbourhood in private homes while our farmhouse became the headquarters. Although we were allowed into the kitchen and pantry, we weren't allowed into the bedroom where Bertha's body was found. Eventually, Mr Priest came over to talk to me.

'G'day to you, Miss Schippan. So we meet once more in tragic circumstances.' I returned his greeting, twiddling my handkerchief and willing myself to remain composed.

'So, Miss, you have returned to Towitta. This is a dreadful business and you must be very distressed. I hope you weren't injured yourself? I'll come and take your evidence as soon as we have organised the men, animals and stores.'

'I'm sure I'll still be here when you need me, Mr Priest. Yes, I remember you from North Adelaide. I came home about six months after Rebekah's death when I was taken ill. And thank you for enquiring about my injuries. I'm not really hurt, just a few cuts and bruises, and I am very tired. My brothers and I are very frightened that the stranger may return; we will not feel safe again until you have found him.'

'Don't you worry, Miss. You are safe now and we will find the murderer, whoever he is.'

It still seems like yesterday. It was hot and dusty. Detective Priest worked his men like soldiers. The troopers were sent in all directions to collect evidence from anyone who was in some way associated with us. They lifted and looked under every movable object as far as the eye could see and collected exhibits that were minutely examined before being arranged and labelled. They scribbled away in notebooks for the inquest.

I sat aside with Mother who had returned by this time. She kept asking me questions and when I wouldn't answer them she cried and sobbed. When I wasn't cooking, washing-up or otherwise helping her I sat on my own and watched everyone rushing about. Father liked to know everything going on about him and wandered about asking the men questions about their work. I saw him and August building an outside fireplace so that Mother and I could help prepare food and drink for the large army of people. We'd never had so many people at the farm at one time.

The mounted troopers brought extra kettles and pans and provisions for the many meals. With the promise of generous payment, Father killed two of his precious sheep each day. There were plenty to choose from but they were pitifully thin and scraggy. This provided mutton which we cooked and ate with potatoes and cabbage and anything that could be found from around the district. Father saw this as an opportunity to earn much-needed cash, more than any of us had seen for a while. It went without saying that Mother and I were expected to be kitchenhands but I didn't mind at all. It kept us busy and took our mind off the reason for their presence in the first place. There were about sixteen policemen, our family of five, and about ten other men who were scientists, journalists and the like. So we spent a lot of time cooking and cleaning up after every meal.

About four o'clock one afternoon, we were rounded up

for a meeting in the implement shed where we listened to the coroner, doctor and detective give their opinions of the events of two nights before. Father was asked again if he had identified Bertha, and he replied in a stern voice that he had. Willy and August, who had earlier sneaked back into the house, spoke morbidly of the pools of dark brown congealed blood, the noisy presence of swarms of blowflies and the awful smell. After agreeing that Bertha's death was due to stab wounds, the inquest was adjourned for nearly a week so that more evidence could be gathered and the case 'worked up', as it was called.

## 16

After Sister Kathleen had gone I slept fitfully, reminded about Bertha's funeral that was to take place the day after the first inquest. By the time Sister Kathleen visited a few days later, I had relived the funeral night after night and felt distressed thinking or telling Sister Kathleen about it. But as usual she had her way of prising from me the stories that had remained locked away for years.

She was cheery and calm and, as always, this soothed my mind. Then she presented me with a small gift. 'Look what I've brought you, Mary. I thought you might like this bottle of scent.'

'Sister, you shouldn't have. It's rather wasted on me for I'll never finish it you know.'

'Now, Mary, I don't want to hear that. You're getting better every day. You tell me these family stories and take my mind away from the home – and frighten me half to death. So it's the least I can do.' And we both laughed, but uncomfortably so.

When we made ourselves comfortable in the enclosed verandah she reminded me that we had planned to talk about Bertha's funeral. She blushed as she said this, suddenly realising that this was an indelicate thing to have said with my own death not far off. She also sensed I was overly tired.

'So how have you been?' she asked, keen to distract me from talk of funerals.

'Not so good, I'm afraid. I am so exhausted. The last time you left I thought about Bertha's funeral and it stayed with me for days, disrupting my sleep. I wish I could forget it but I can't. So I'd better tell you about it, so it will leave my mind. But I do find it distressing talking about undertakers and funerals.'

'You really don't have to go through this, Mary.'

I've been reliving this for days, so I may as well tell you about it. I told you about the first inquest. The undertaker came the next morning as the funeral was in the Sedan cemetery in the afternoon. Mother was given permission to prepare Bertha's body which had been laid out on her bed by Mrs Lambert. I was too nervy to help her and she never pressed me to do so. Bertha was dressed in her Sunday frock with one of Mother's old lace collars wrapped around her neck to cover the gaping wounds. When the undertaker arrived in the morning he placed Bertha in a simple black painted coffin.

We all dressed up in our Sunday clothes for Bertha's funeral. Father wanted Bertha in the coffin to be on display in the yard before we travelled to Sedan so everyone in the family and nearby neighbours could see her, if they wished. This was a Wendish tradition and was very important to Father and Mother and all our relatives. So after much discussion with Detective Priest Father had his way, despite the dreadful furnace-like conditions and the way in which Bertha had been brutally murdered by a stranger. I had not seen Bertha since her death and had no wish to look at her now she was placed on view. I found it too morbid. I think when Mother said that Bertha's face was as pale as a ghost, it really upset me.

Being a Wendish coffin, the sides were folded down to show off the body but there was no sign to suggest how she had died. The troopers helped to keep the affair private. They fenced off a small area near one of the barns with posts and ropes so that it was difficult for anyone casually passing by the farm to see Bertha's coffin from the roadway.

Our aunties and uncles arrived throughout the morning and joined us for an early lunch. Despite the intense summer heat, they had journeyed from Mount Pleasant, Eden Valley, Springton and Angaston to give us support for the funeral. Even my oldest brother Frederick had come back under the protection of one of the uncles from Eden Valley. Father and he had not spoken since the day he had left home, and despite the tragic circumstances Father refused to speak to him still. Frederick told me he was not in the least upset by this.

The coffin was transported in the undertaker's carriage while Mother and Father followed. Frederick, Willy, August and I sat in the Matschoss's cart; they were our neighbours. We always called Mrs Matschoss Aunt Martha because she was Mother's closest friend. Several other families followed behind as we wended our way over the dusty roads in the face of a stinging gritty wind to the cemetery at Sedan. I could hear Mother sobbing and when I looked round I saw my aunties were weeping too, dabbing at their eyes with handkerchiefs. Willy and August, who hardly spoke, had blank expressions on their faces like funeral mutes. They showed no distress whatsoever.

When we arrived at the windswept graveyard, enclosed by a low concrete wall and topped with barbed wire, a crowd of men trickled out of the nearby public house to look at the passing cortege. They removed their hats out of respect. No one needed to move closer for a look as the ceremony could be clearly seen from the pub's shady verandah.

The ceremony at the graveside was painful. The service conducted by Pastor Schaerer was only minutes long for it was still over a hundred degrees in the shade. He was assisted by Pastor Heidenreich of Bethany. Father supported Mother, but I just clutched my only white lace hankie and dabbed my dry eyes. It was difficult for me to believe what was happening. I did not feel part of the funeral; it seemed to be taking place while I watched, distant and disconnected. The wind was so strong that the pastors' voices were sometimes blown away.

When Bertha's coffin was lowered into the ground and covered with the sandy dirt, the publican, Mr Meyer, his wife and other helpers brought trays of cold water and cordial for us to drink. Mother was at breaking point and beyond noticing what was happening around her, but Father seemed deeply touched by this kindly gesture, especially as he had a healthy dislike of public houses. Mrs Meyer gave Mother a comforting embrace and said, 'We are all so sorry for you, Mrs Schippan.'

At these few simple words, Mother collapsed in tears and had to be lifted back onto the wagon. The rest of us followed and returned to Towitta at a brisk trot, despite the intense heat. No one spoke. Every now and again when there was a lull in the wind, Mother's pitiful sobbing reached us. I clenched my jaw, looked straight ahead and thought of happier times spent in Adelaide and with Gustave.

Back at Towitta, Mother and I made tea, producing sliced cake for those few relatives who returned home with us. There was little talk. No one knew what to say without someone breaking down in tears. An auntie spoke to reassure me, 'Now look here, Mary, the murderer will soon be caught and you'll have nothing more to fear.' There was much concern that I was in shock, terrified of the intruder turning up again. I said nothing.

Having told Sister Kathleen about Bertha's funeral, it seemed there was nothing more to be said. I felt exhausted.

'Let me help you, Mary,' and Sister Kathleen led me inside and put me to bed.

## 17

It was about a fortnight before I saw Sister Kathleen again. She had spent her annual holiday at home in the Barossa Valley with her parents. Every night after she left me, I would have worrying dreams. Nightmares had not plagued me for more than seven years following Father's death, but now I began to dream about the stories I was telling her. Sister Kathleen was keen to hear the end of the story and she was determined I should continue. When she returned from the Barossa she brought me jam and biscuits that her mother had made. I thanked her and we reminded ourselves where my story had finished. I told her it was at the first inquest, and we made ourselves comfortable on the verandah.

The days dragged by after the funeral. In the following week, on the Thursday morning, the second inquest took place. All this time the wind had blown without letting up and the heat was like that coming from a baker's oven. In the night before the inquest the wind dropped and it rained lightly, but this only made conditions heavy and sultry. The temperature remained high and unpleasant.

As we hadn't been allowed to sleep in the house since Bertha's death, we camped in the small shed where Father stored his tools and machinery, while August and Willy shared their barn with several troopers. That morning, as usual, our family ate breakfast together sitting on benches and logs outside. We waited to be called over to the largest barn where a courtroom was once more set up for an inquest. This time it seemed hundreds of people from all around the district had turned up to see what they could learn firsthand about Bertha. It was unnerving to see so many local people walking about on our farm, virtually where they liked.

Mr Cockburn, a keen journalist from the *Register* news-paper, arrived for the inquest in an automobile. This became the main attraction for the locals; many of them had never before seen a motor car. I was told it was a Lewis model that had been hired from its proud Adelaide owner. It was driven by Mr O'Grady who rushed the messages relating to the inquest to Angaston. From there they were telegraphed to Mr Cockburn's newspaper office in Adelaide. We were told it was the very first automobile ever used by a newspaper in South Australia.

News of the motor's arrival in the district spread rapidly. German farmers arrived and discussed the new form of trans-port with admiration and envy. August told me that some of the farmers saw it flying through the countryside at between twenty and thirty miles per hour. One farmer reported he had actually seen it jump the Rhine Creek, from one bank to the other. At the time the creek was nothing more than a dry sandy hollow in the road. Farmers hung around for hours, seem-ingly with nothing better to do. They laughed and chattered, spending their time inspecting and touching the motor.

There were other means for newspapers to race their news from Towitta to the telegraph office in Angaston, or directly to Adelaide. Each day bicycles were ridden up the treacherous hills to Angaston by some of the best cyclists in the state. There were horses and riders and a man with carrier pigeons that flew directly to Adelaide.

After dawn and before the inquest got underway, I rinsed out some clothes and was hanging them on the washing line when Mr Cockburn asked me whether I wouldn't mind giving him my thoughts about the events the week before. Naturally enough I was wary about saying anything but he was deter-mined I should be interviewed and he reassured me it was for the public interest. I obliged.

'Did your sister not wake when you were scuffling with the man?' He made notes as I spoke.

'Oh yes. She was awake and calling out "August".'

'Did she get out of bed?'

'No, I don't think she did.'

'How long did your struggle last?'

'About ten minutes, I should think.'

'Did you call for your sister?'

'No, I called for August.'

'Could she not have helped you?' he asked, looking puzzled.

'I don't think she got out of bed while I was in the room.'

'Had your assailant any beard?'

'I don't know, it was too dark to see.'

'What sort of a coat – holland or tweed, rough or smooth – did he wear?'

'I don't know, I couldn't see.'

'But you did feel his clothes?'

'Yes, it was a rough felt.' He was silent while he recorded this information.

'Why did your sister not run through your mother's bedroom while you were struggling?'

'I don't know; I thought that myself.'

'What clothes did you wear in bed?'

'A blouse, chemise, and stockings.'

'You put your skirt on as you ran to your brother's room for help?'

'Yes.'

'How long was your brother away at Henke's?'

'About half an hour.'

'When he returned without Henke, you all came to the house. What did you do?'

I answered in detail, 'We listened outside and then called Bertha but we heard nothing. We had pitchforks and a rifle so we went into the kitchen and lit the lamp. The door leading to our bedroom had been closed after I ran out earlier. As we were about to open the door we were suddenly afraid to go inside, so I blew out the lamp, and we all ran as fast as we could over to Lambert, the constable's place. We were gone about half an hour, I should think. They would not get up quickly, because they did not believe us at first. Then he came back with us.'

'Did you see your sister's body?'

'No, I have not seen her at all since.'

'During the half an hour your brother was gone to Henke's, you stayed in your brothers' room in the barn?'

'Yes.'

Our talk was very matter of fact and he seemed pleased by what I told him. He wrote what I said word for word in the newspapers and gave us a copy of several of them later. I still have the cuttings which I have read many times since. I had told that story of the event several times by then, I knew it word for word. And after all, telling stories was what I was good at.

After Mr Cockburn interviewed me he set up his fancy camera on a tripod and took photographs of me on my own. He also took them of me with my parents and brothers. Father had been reassured it was for the public interest and Mr Cockburn said he would make sure we got copies of the photographs of our family at a later date. I thought that was wonderful. We had never had any photographs taken in our family before, for we could not afford a camera or a photographer. He then went off and took pictures of the farm from all angles and of all the officials as they worked.

Father was angry when he discovered Mr Cockburn had interviewed me on my own before the outcome of the inquest.

'What do you mean, my girl, by allowing yourself to be on your own with him. I don't think he had any right to ask you questions without me or your mother being present. Who knows what he will put in the papers. What will people think? This will do you no good, my girl.' Father said Mr Cockburn took great liberties with us all. We heard later that photographers were banned from taking pictures at the scene of a crime, of witnesses, suspects or inquests.

Mother said that the officials had begun the day by having

breakfast at William Mulligan's house before the inquest took place at our farm. At around nine in the morning they arrived and our family was called to the barn and told where to sit. Just as I sat down I caught Gustave's eye and my heart missed a beat. I hadn't thought that he'd be there as a witness. I hadn't seen him for about ten days and now I wondered if all this trouble had broken our relationship for good. He was there for one reason only. Someone must have told of our affair. Surely they would not pry into our private business, the kind of things you don't talk about? What would that have to do with Bertha's death?

Gustave was sitting on the other side of the barn with a trooper and the sun filtered through the slats in the palings making his hair glint. When our eyes met he bowed his head and fiddled with his hat. I could see he was uncomfortable. I did not see him look in my direction again. This unsettled me for I could not gain friendly reassurance from him either by eye movement or smile. What tales was he going to tell? I felt my face flush and I wanted to die with shame at what he might say about us.

The many people who couldn't fit inside the overflowing barn hung about outside, many lingered around the motor. As I was close to one of the gaps in the walls, I strained to listen to what was being said by those crowded by the automobile and those listening through the palings. When someone outside couldn't hear properly, those who could passed on the latest facts as they heard them. Through the cracks I could see much nodding and shaking of heads, grimaces and scratching of heads, pulling of beards and sucking on old smelly pipes by the knowing crowd.

'What he say?' one asked.

'He said it was the stab to the back of the neck that killed her.'

About eighteen witnesses were called and the questions and answers went on hour after hour all day. Most of those who came to hear what was going on stayed all day fearing they'd miss some sensation if they left early. Some brought picnic hampers and at lunchtime locals sat together and shared their food. During lunch, while Mother and Father returned to the little shed to eat, I was taken over to our house and made to eat with Mr Mulligan and Detective Priest who said not a word throughout the meal break. I was surprised at being separated from the rest of the family.

The inquest stopped at dusk when the light faded. Next morning it continued as it had the day before. It was on this day that Gustave revealed to the public the most intimate details of our private affair and I was to be questioned too. I was shocked about this, but thankfully, before I provided private details of our friendship, Mr Foster, my lawyer from Kapunda, said I was not on trial and need not respond to these questions. So I didn't. By this time Gustave had said it all anyway. What was there left to say?

When the questioning finally turned to Bertha's death I started talking, 'I woke to find a man on the bed lying across me with his head over my sister. The blade of the knife caught my arm when he grabbed hold of one of my wrists. I struggled out of bed bumping myself very heavily against the sewing machine. As I fought him I heard the knife falling and, in that instant, I dashed for the door in the pitch black. I grabbed hold of a skirt hanging on the back of a door and ran out the kitchen door screaming for my brothers. I was terrified.'

The questioning went on for hours about whether I was wearing a blue or pink blouse, because one of them had been found in pieces covered in blood. They wanted to catch me out on this fact of whether it was a blue or pink blouse. What did it matter? It was some time before I was permitted to sit down again.

In the late afternoon Dr Steel spoke of Bertha's death from a doctor's point of view. He went into scientific details of knife size and so on, looking my way for a response. I looked straight past him, never allowing a flinch or flicker of an eyelash. I knew if I let him into my mind, I might swoon. He spoke about how Bertha had been slaughtered like an animal and I couldn't believe anyone could do such a barbaric act. Yet I was supposed to have been there when the deed took place. Of course I hadn't seen a thing, it being in the dark. But I was there. I felt it happening but because it was pitch black, my imagination was making the pictures I couldn't see. So afterwards I wonder about what I know and what I imagined.

Then the questions were over and the officials huddled together comparing notes. My heart pounded and I hardly dared to take breath in the stifling heat. I sat rigid holding my only handkerchief. Several minutes passed while I watched someone produce a batch of papers and put them in some order in front of Mr Mulligan. Mr Foster leaned over and said I must go and stand in front of the bench being used as the jury table. This unnerved me. I wondered why only I had to stand in front of everyone. There was a hush as Mr Mulligan, looking very severe, stared straight into my eyes and announced, 'We, the Jury, are of opinion that Bertha Elizabeth Schippan met her death on the first night of January, 1902, by having her throat cut by Mary Augusta Schippan. She stands charged before the undersigned, one of his Majesty's justices of the peace, that at Towitta, she did feloniously, wilfully and of her malice aforethought, kill and murder Bertha Schippan.' After two days of general questions and answers in friendly terms, what Mr Mulligan now said was imprinted into my memory forever.

There was a gasp of dismay from everyone in the shed. Then there was a noisy rush for the exit by journalists, keen to be the first to relay their telegraphs to Adelaide. I could see out between the palings of the barn as people scrambled for their bikes, horses and to release the carrier pigeons. And this included the driver and the Lewis car.

After such dreadful accusations and with all eyes on me, I wanted to swoon away. But I could not move from the spot. My story about the intruder had been ignored when I thought everyone believed me. As Father listened to the outcome I saw his hands pulling on his grey beard and his brow deeply furrowed. It must have been grim for him and Mother to hear that their last living daughter must now stand trial for the murder of her younger sister. Father's gaunt face was fixed, not a muscle moved except for the nervous twitching of his eyes. And as I looked at Mother, I saw the light in her eyes dim. I think I must have gone into one of my daydreams at that moment for what was being said around me drifted into the background and was like a din somewhere far off.

My life now took a new direction. For several days up to this moment everyone had rushed around collecting evidence and making pages of notes while being friendly toward me. For days I brewed endless cups of tea and baked numerous German cakes. No one ever refused when I topped up their tin mugs or offered a slice of cake. But all niceties towards me stopped when Mr Mulligan read the statement accusing me.

The event of a week ago was like an awful nightmare that hadn't ended when I woke at the Lambert's house, but had continued when the barn was converted to a courtroom. Now I had been committed to trial for the murder of Bertha I realised there had been no nightmare at all. But it made no sense to me. Someone took hold of my arm and I came back to my senses. The voices became louder once more and someone was calling my name but I couldn't respond, like I was half asleep.

As the statement was read, Father pressed forward nervously. Immediately the warrant was read and signed I was told to sit down. The inquest was over. The noise in the courtroom had reached fever pitch, but no one left except the journalists. The air was hot, sticky and pungent from the many people packed into a small space for hours in the Australian summer heat. Mr Mulligan hushed the crowd and told everyone, 'Sisters and brothers, the inquest is over. There is nothing else for anyone to see so you'd better all go home.'

After a few minutes, the crowds began leaving. As they filed past me, I sensed for the first time a new and knowing look, a look both unsettling and hostile. Some people, whom I had known for years, hissed like snakes as they passed me. One whispered so only I could hear, 'Murderer, whore.' Someone spat at me. I was no longer left alone. After all, I was under arrest for murder and maybe they believed I was at risk of acting that way again if I wasn't watched. They must believe I was now more dangerous than ten minutes before. I might bolt or suddenly produce a knife and kill them all. I was now closely guarded when walking from the barn to the farmhouse, past a crowd that had formed to watch me pass. As I walked across the yard Willy and August stood aside to let us pass and I saw them staring hard at me in utter disbelief with tears streaming down their faces. I also saw their fear.

## 18

# Wilhelm and August Schippan

*11 January 1902*

As Mary passed, Willy grabbed August's arm and sobbed, 'Why did she do it, August?'

August couldn't answer him and he was uncertain about what was going to happen to her now – or them for that matter. Before that fateful night they had endured a scorching and miserable Christmas with their mother and father before their parents left for a few days without them. They all wanted to cry from disappointment, the children rarely had an opportunity to leave the farm. Bertha had made their lives a trial. She hounded Mary about not being able to go to the New Year's Eve dance at Sedan which was seven miles away. Their father did not approve of dances, and it would have meant travelling along the roads on their own without an adult to chaperone. The only person who could have accompanied them was Mary's sweetheart Gustave, but he had gone to Adelaide the day before. There was no point to Bertha carrying on, Father's word was law and that was that. Mary would be thrashed if they disobeyed her.

It wasn't worth the risk of a hiding. They were already covered in bruises and lash marks that they'd received through the weeks leading up to Christmas. They could see that their parents had little spare money to spend on Christmas and their mother told them they had to make sacrifices this year. She tried to cheer them by saying she would make amends when their circumstances had improved with a middle-of-the-year Christmas dinner, a goose perhaps.

Christmas Day for them was little different to any other day for they had the same baked mutton and spuds. A steamed pudding of sorts was the only treat. There were no special German cakes and puddings that they had so looked forward to. It didn't help that the heat was at its worst and the nights were stifling. When August and Willy finished the usual chores they walked to the shade of Cowlands Creek to get away from their father. The heat was so intense they simply lay down on the banks of the creek with their guns and catapults, too overcome to move or even to speak. Earlier they had spoken of running away to join their older brothers as soon as they could pluck up the courage. August had promised to send a note to see whether their brothers would come and collect them.

Over the Christmas period Mary's sweetheart Gustave hung about until the afternoon he headed off to Adelaide with his team of horses and wagon. August and Willy didn't mind him visiting because he reminded them of their older brothers who showed them how to do handy jobs. He never ceased to impress them with his skill at managing six powerful horses. Sometimes when he left the farm they would travel some miles with him just so they could have the chance of driving the horses themselves. He trusted them too. He would give one of them the reins of the wonderful creatures and head for the back of the cart where he lay down on some sacking and whistled or sang with his hat covering his face. And the horses did what they told them when Gustave showed them how.

Everyone, it seems, wanted Gustave's attention when he was about, so good-natured was he. Bertha would draw him out on things she wanted to know about Adelaide or about his job. And even exhausted Mary would perk up a little when Gustave was about. They soon noticed that he always wanted to put his arms about her when he thought no one was watching. She thought they never saw her and Gustave together, but they spied on them often. Willy kept asking August if Mary would have a baby. They knew they behaved like married people did, although Mother and Father had long since ceased any shows of affection. They were keen to see where this hugging and cuddling would lead and what their father would do if he ever found out what was going on in the barn at the weekends or in their home over Christmas. Then Gustave drove off to Adelaide.

On the first day of the year Mary told Bertha to go and play with Violet and Ella at the Henkes' place, and stop hanging around like a hungry blowfly. Willy and August took off in the morning for the day, heading to one of the creeks with their guns and enough food tied up in one of their father's old sacks. They intended shooting a few parrots and galahs for a stew and finding some wood for whittling with their sharpest knives. They liked carving such creatures as dwarfs or animals from mallee roots.

They were so carried away with their day out that it was evening when they arrived home. Mary gave them warm tea and cake, because they were so worn out from their activities and the heat of the day, then gave them the only lamp which they took to their beds in the shed. It didn't take them long to fall asleep.

It seemed they'd hardly fallen asleep when Mary burst into the barn later that night screaming. They couldn't see her until August lit the lamp. Her wild eyes and her unkempt hair made her look as though their worst nightmares had come true, that a wicked witch had come to kidnap them. It took some time for her to convince them that she was indeed their sister Mary, so awful did she look in the lamplight. By this time Willy was hysterical and didn't know what to believe when Mary told them that an intruder was in the house with Bertha. Mary sent August to seek help from Ferdy Henke, and she stayed hidden with Willy in the barn.

August worried when Willy told him afterwards about their time in the barn. He was scared out of his wits by what Mary said. She told Willy that if he didn't do as he was told and be quiet, the intruder would find them both and slit their throats too. Long after the murder August wondered why Mary continued to frighten Willy. She repeated to him that the man was still out there somewhere and could come and find them anytime he chose.

August had never been sure about Mary. They were both a little afraid of her, perhaps because she was so often cold and distant. Many a time he had seen her slaughter a sheep or a pig and wring a fowl's neck with no effort, but he simply didn't believe she was strong enough to murder Bertha. Bertha was as big as them and much stronger than Mary. However, August had seen Mary find a super strength when it suited her.

On the day after the murder, in their continuing search to understand death, August and Willy sneaked into the house while the police were eating dinner and closely studied Bertha. Her eyes were open. They prodded her and whispered to her but she didn't respond. August had to calm Willy when he failed to waken her. He told him to be brave and keep quiet until they could get away to somewhere more private.

# 19

## Mary

When Sister Kathleen dropped by after she had finished her rounds one morning, she brought me half a fruit cake, baked by her mother.

'Come, Mary, let's sit under the trees for a chat and eat the cake there.'

'How was your holiday? You went home didn't you?'

'It was a pleasant rest from this mad house, I can tell you. But my father was hobbling about in pain more than usual. His leg never really recovered from the accident he had when I was a little girl.'

'What happened?' It was my chance to hear a story.

'When Father was publican in Angaston, his leg was almost smashed to pieces in a freak accident. It happened during the weekly beer delivery from the brewery. Father was in the cellar when several kegs accidently fell through the cellar opening. One of the brewery horses shied for some reason. We all thought Father had been killed. Fred, 'the boots', as publicans call their odd-job men, saved his life by dragging him from beneath the kegs and up the steps to the trap. He rushed him off to the German hospital where Mother's brother-in-law worked as a limb-maker. Mother had to take over the pub but next morning, being Saturday and no school, she drove my brother and me to see him. I'll never forget it for I expected to find my father dying. Instead he was sitting up in bed laughing and carrying on with three young wounded soldiers from the Boer War and a nurse, all in white. Well, I'd never seen anyone like her before. She looked like an angel in her white starched uniform. She was taking their temperatures and telling these four grown men how to behave. And guess what, Mary?'

'What?'

'They all took notice of her. I also saw her dressing the wound of the stump of the leg of one of them. And though I was only a little girl, that's when I decided to become a nurse. This was about the same time my father was told that his younger brother had died of gunshot wounds to his stomach while fighting in South Africa. Father said his brother was always a bit of a larrikin but joined up for adventure. It was so long before he was given medical attention that he died.'

'How sad.'

'It was. But like many families there were plenty of animosities within it. You see, Aunty's German family supported the Boers' cause in South Africa. It seems that when my uncle's grandfather first came to South Australia, he felt hard done by when he was not allowed to register as a doctor. But he became one anyway, practising at first in a small way as a homeopathic practitioner. He was also well known for mending bones or replacing missing limbs because that's what he'd done when he was in the Prussian army before he came to South Australia. But he never forgot how he was treated and when the South African war began, he caused a lot of problems by letting it be known whose side he was on. Despite all that, he never turned anyone away from his hospital.'

She looked away as she gathered her breath. 'So, your turn, tell me what happened after the inquest and how you were treated once you had been accused of being a murderess.'

I'll never forget the fear in August and Willy's eyes when I was led to the farmhouse by two policemen after the inquest. I was told I was going to Adelaide as soon as I had taken some refreshment and packed a bag. It had never occurred to me that this would happen, that I would leave Towitta so suddenly. For so long I had yearned to go, but not like this. Sitting on the scrubbed wooden table in the kitchen was a large pot of tea and a fruit loaf. Mother was laid out with grief on the kitchen sofa and her loud sobs intensified when she saw me in the company of the troopers. She rushed to me and clung, sobbing, 'But you're my only girl now … and they are taking you from me.'

When I finished eating, I gathered clothes into a bag and kissed my sobbing mother goodbye. She staggered outside after me, Father supporting her. 'I did not do it, Mother,' I reassured her calmly.

Father watched me closely while she replied, 'I know you didn't, girl.' And the sobbing began afresh. 'I have lost two daughters at once. I have lost them all.'

At the sight of my bewildered parents, the hot tears fell. They were the first tears I had shed since Bertha's death. I climbed into one of the police carriages that was to transport me to the Angaston police station with constables Beckmann and Campbell. I cried a good deal of the way to Angaston. The two policemen didn't know how to comfort me. Their attempts were clumsy but well-meaning, 'Now c'mon, Miss, it's not as bad as all that. You've got nothing to worry about you know … if you didn't do it.'

Of course these reassuring words only made me cry louder. Then through sheer weariness and relief, I fell asleep. Sometime after midnight we arrived in Angaston and I was shaken awake and taken to the cells behind the police station. I was exhausted, my head throbbed and my face was swollen from the crying. After having the charge of murder read out to me again, I was told I'd be taken by horse and carriage to Freeling where we'd catch the steam train to Adelaide. After a few hours sleep on a narrow creaking bed, I was roused before dawn and told to prepare myself for the journey. I put back on my black dress. Because it was so early in the morning and a little chilly, I took my brown cape from my bag and brushed my hair as best as I could without a mirror. When I washed my face in a bowl of cool water I felt better, though my eyes felt puffy and my head still ached.

I climbed into the coach and nearly broke into fresh tears when I found the assistant crown solicitor and the coroner seated inside. A small crowd of people had gathered to see us off. I was happy to hide behind the veil that Mother gave me, from both the crowd outside and the crown solicitor and the coroner within, who glanced my way knowingly. They sat opposite each other and seemed immersed in their discussions, but now and again Dr Ramsay Smith, the coroner, would stare at me but say nothing. When we arrived at Freeling railway station our group sat on the platform, waiting for the morning express train from Kapunda. I sat on a bench under the verandah, the station basking in the early morning sun, not yet burning. Only Constable Beckmann now travelled with me. Dressed in plain clothes, he sat some distance away in order not to attract attention to me.

While I waited, a two-year-old who had travelled with her mother on the coach to Freeling approached me in a friendly manner. She was so endearing I spilled a tear or two, realising it was unlikely that I would ever have a darling girl like her to call my own. When the train steamed in twenty minutes later I took my place like an ordinary passenger, off to Adelaide for shopping or a visit, in a second-class compartment with the constable seated nearby. During the journey others boarded but the policeman gave no indication that he was with me, and the other passengers were oblivious to my state. If only you knew who I was, I thought, the alleged Towitta murderess, no less. How would you treat me then? Would you move out of the carriage if you knew, or spit in my eye with outrage? But no one guessed; no one even looked in my direction.

When the train arrived at Gawler station I saw a group of people marching up and down the platform inspecting the passengers, hoping to catch a glimpse of the alleged murderess, I guessed. But they were fooled by the plain-clothes policeman who made a show of being oblivious to me and when the train started again for Adelaide, I never felt their curious eyes on me for a moment.

## 20

At this point, a nurse called for Sister Kathleen to help and she did not return. It was three days before I saw her again.

'Hallo there,' she said, as she poked her head around the door. 'Can I come in? I'm sorry about the other day but it can be so busy some days when there aren't enough staff for the work. The staff are falling like ninepins, struck down by the influenza that's raging. Do you know, Mary, countless people are dying from it? An emergency hospital has been established at the Jubilee Hall to quarantine people.' She settled into a chair near my bed. 'Time to move from one depressing topic to another.'

'You mean prison? Now, Sister, I've guessed your curiosity about my imprisonment and the time has come to tell you how it was. It was supposed to be a place of punishment, but the truth is it was one of the happiest times in my life.'

When the train reached North Adelaide Station, I was led to a waiting horse and trap. By lunchtime I'd passed through the sallyport of the Adelaide Gaol. As I passed through I heard the clanking of the keys as this inner iron gate locked behind me and it would be two months before I was once again to pass through those gates to stand trial. The prison was cold and dank, a stark contrast to the hot bright world outside.

I was unprepared for the terror of being locked alone in a cell each night, where the black was so like my nightmares that it affected my sanity. I was told that at the time there were no other women prisoners on remand, so I joined the convicted women prisoners. They knew about me and the story of what I had done, and they assured me I would be shown no mercy but be hanged like Elizabeth Woolcock, nearly twenty-five years before. They reminded me that nothing saved her from the gallows after she'd poisoned her brutal husband, even though many believed she had reasonable grounds for doing so. To shock me I was told that her body, as with all those executed at the prison, was buried between the walls of the prison. The frenzied stabbing, which they were convinced I did, was the act of a madwoman who deserved the ultimate punishment.

They taunted me. 'Are you mad, Mary Schippan?' they asked, every day. I was reminded that there was no likelihood of a lesser punishment, that hanging was inevitable for a frenzied killer and the charge would not be downgraded to a manslaughter charge. They mocked my hope of a miracle that would see me acquitted. 'Who believes in miracles?' they asked. I told them it was a ghastly mistake, at which they broke out into howls of laughter stating, 'That's what we all say, Mary Schippan, but as you can see no one believed us either.'

A well-known woman of the night told me, 'Mary Schippan, I have been to this prison more times than you've had cream cakes, and not one of us has ever admitted her crime. So we're all innocent too.' They cackled and laughed like a flock of corellas, but despite all their carry-on I knew it was a terrible mistake and I would be acquitted when the intruder was caught. But despite my fragile confidence I carried a sense of dread about my trial. The outcome of the inquest had been so unexpected; perhaps I must prepare myself for never leaving prison alive.

I was jailed in a three-storey wing of the prison that housed about fifty convicted women prisoners. I mixed with prostitutes, abortionists, pickpockets and drunks. Most were good-natured despite their mockery of me. They didn't hold out hope for me because they believed I had committed a brutal crime, not like their minor crimes of petty thieving or indecent language. My prospects were not good, as they never ceased to remind me, but they soon treated me as one of their own and included me in their activities.

Although I was petrified of the dark and anxious of the outcome of my trial, I felt liberated in a strange way. I was away from Towitta and more importantly, I was away from Father, and I had the company of the women throughout the day. The nights remained terrifying. The lonely dark led to new and terrible nightmares. Barely a speck of light penetrated the blackness once the heavy wooden door was locked on me. Yet I stayed awake because of the early hour. During the long black nights the border dividing nightmare and reality blurred. I had been troubled for many years by the nightmare of the goblin sitting on my chest, but from my first night in prison I had a new nightmare. It was a dream wrapped inside another. I thought I'd woken from it only to find I hadn't, and the nightmare would continue on its twisted way.

I dreamt my clothes were covered in warm sticky blood after I chopped off the heads of animals. The blood, more than any parrot, pig or sheep could possibly spill, sprayed over my face, my hair and my feet. Then I woke inside another dream but it was not parrots' blood spurting over me this time but Bertha's. I screamed inside my night terror. I couldn't see the blood for it was pitch black but I could feel it warm and sticky as I slid across the kitchen floor and Bertha was laughing hysterically at me. The parrot's head that became a pig's head became Bertha's. I screamed for my life.

The nights I had a reprieve from this nightmare, I returned to my childhood one of waking, paralysed, to find a goblin-like creature sitting on my chest – the changeling, the strange intruder. Wasn't this what happened to me on the night of the murder when I found the stranger lying across me attacking Bertha?

My blood-curdling screams invariably woke the women. They yelled curses at me to keep quiet. This sometimes brought the warden to see what the din was about. She'd tell me not to be so childish, that they were silly nightmares. She thought I was screaming because I was frightened of the intruder who I said murdered Bertha. But I never saw him in my nightmares.

Most of the prisoners were so kind and friendly that I

wondered why they were there. Sometimes a woman's children were also locked up, at the Magill Reform Institute, or fostered out, for there was no husband or family member to look after them. Several women worried about their poor little motherless children growing up in some cheerless institution or in an unkind foster home. There were plenty of tales being spread about the cruel foster homes.

The women grew flowers and vegetables around the prison yards and were allowed to knit, sew, tat and quilt. We were sometimes allowed to walk for exercise and some of the women carved pretty little scrimshaw-like pictures into the hard red bricks of the inner walls of the prison when no one was watching. Flowers and birds and images of the natural world that we missed were beautifully scratched into the bricks. I scratched a picture of a vase of flowers. Another woman carved a sailing ship like the one she'd sailed on to South Australia many years before.

I worked as hard as they did and I soon made friends. We worked from breakfast until teatime at five o'clock. After tea we were locked up again. The women did all the laundry for the Adelaide Hospital, the washing and the ironing. We often spent our afternoons in a vast room at a long table sewing the clothes we had to wear, as well as clothes for the male prisoners. The wardens were surprisingly relaxed and we were allowed to talk while we worked. Only when the language became too coarse were we reprimanded.

Each Sunday we trooped into the chapel for a religious service. It was on the first floor of the two-storey building at the entrance of the prison. We were separated from the men by a wooden partition, but we could see them through the cracks. I don't know why we bothered but because we could see the men and we assumed they could see us, we all took care to preen ourselves before we visited the chapel.

We had some kindly regular visitors. Each week Caroline Maughan, a grand old lady from the Methodist Church, visited us for two hours or so in the sewing room. She brought us comfort and hope. She was the widow of a well-known minister and she was kind and gentle, which had a wondrous calming effect on us. She listened to our fears and hopes for the future without condemning our behaviour. All bad language stopped when she was in our midst.

I was allowed a special visitor from the Lutheran Church in Adelaide. Pastor Eitel, not much older than me, visited every week. I eagerly anticipated seeing him. Like Mrs Maughan he gave us reason to believe that our stay in prison would be brief. But while Mrs Maughan visited us all, Pastor Eitel was my own special visitor. I told him of my nightmares, but his calming words did not stop them.

When we sat together in little groups to sew I responded to the other women's queries about my nightmares. I spoke about my life with Father and the fairytales we told each other at home which invariably frightened us to death. Of course they were curious about the more bizarre Wendish fairy-tales which I knew were capable of frightening adults. Some of the more popular tales about Cinderella, Rapunzel and Rumpelstiltskin they knew, but they had never heard of 'The Girl with no Hands', 'How the Children Played Butchers', or even 'Bluebeard'. So I became a popular storyteller, the best they'd known. So around the sewing tables in the afternoon they would hush each other when they wanted me to begin a story. I would tell them about the Wendish witches and the ter-rible Waterman who drowned children by enticing them into lakes, rivers or water tanks. Even Mrs Maughan was shaken by the violence of some of the fairytales.

'Miss Schippan, I don't think your fairytales are proper. Fairytales are meant to be for children not for you women.'

'Yeah, but aren't Mary's more thrilling – more real?' one of the women said on my behalf.

Their favourite story was about the time I ran after a tree spirit in the Towitta Creek, and as he slipped down between the crevices of a rivergum root my fingers caught hold of his clothing. Long after he vanished my fingers glowed an eerie green in the dark. I asked the women to snuff out the candles or cover the windows to darken the room so they could see my fingers glowing green like fireflies in the darkened room. Showing them this trick never ceased to amaze them. They had no idea how it was done. And I was not about to enlighten them for it would destroy my standing among them. It never occurred to them that the copper coin I held in my hand and which I was rubbing vigorously into my hot sweaty hand, was creating the magic. Father had shown us this trick when we were young but it took many years to figure out how it was done. I was only able to tell the tree spirit story and undertake the trick after finding a copper penny in one of the vegetable gardens and hiding it in my pinafore. A couple of the older women were unnerved at this trick and thought me a witch, or something even more sinister. They were quite frightened of me and kept their distance.

All too quickly the remand period, one of the best times in my life, came to an end. It was March and the trial was to begin.

# 21

## Detective Priest

### 16 January 1902

It came as no surprise to Priest when the inquest ordered Mary Schippan to stand trial. He'd hoped it might be her cruel father but there was no evidence to indicate it could be him. Once Mary was committed for trial, the matter of exhuming the body of Bertha became imperative. There needed to be a search for clues that implicated Mary, clues that may have been missed during the initial examination.

The government coroner, Dr Ramsay Smith, wanted to carry out his own investigations. So only a few days after the official inquest, having returned to Adelaide and disbanded the troops and equipment, Priest and an assistant accompanied Dr Smith back to the godforsaken country at Sedan to exhume the body of Bertha. When they eventually arrived at the Sedan cemetery they erected tarpaulins over the grave while the coffin was dug up. It was a gruesome affair seeing this beautiful young girl once more. Smith used a razor-sharp scalpel to scrape under Bertha's nails and the specimens, including long light-brown hairs, were placed into a box. Dr Ramsay Smith proceeded to undertake further detailed examinations.

Priest looked puzzled. 'Sir, I'm trying to get a clear picture of what went on between these sisters. I know Bertha was very unhappy about not being allowed to go to the New Year's Eve dance in the Sedan Institute. Maybe she was planning to meet a young man there?'

'Or maybe the accused's sweetheart looked in the direction of this girl. You know, jealousy, revenge and so on. It's all here somewhere. If there are clues that we can't find now, then they will return to this grave.'

Priest asked, 'Have you finished for now, Sir'.

Ramsay Smith replied, 'I have, Priest, so we'll cover the grave again and take the box of specimens to the hotel. I'll ask the landlord to lock them up for us while we stay the night. Then we'll make an early start in the morning for Adelaide.'

# 22

# Mary

One evening about five days later, Sister Kathleen appeared at the start of her night shift. She promised she'd return later that evening when the hospital was quiet. I was in bed when she reappeared and she lit the lamp, settled in a chair by my bed and I continued the story as I remembered it.

On the night before the trial began, I was taken to a small room next to the sheriff's office where my lawyer, Mr Anthony Foster from Kapunda, was waiting to speak with me. With him he had another lawyer, the smartest in town I was assured. Mr Josiah Symon came forward to greet me when I entered the room. He asked me to sit and he told me about himself and what he expected of me the next morning in court. He gushed with confidence.

'You are fortunate, Miss Schippan. Your lawyer, Mr Foster, went to great lengths to retain me for you. Eighty pounds has been raised in and around Sedan and Angaston by a local farmer, Abraham Shannon, to pay the legal costs.'

Of course I knew this name because he was once the local district council chairman and had a large farm, but I'd never met him. I was surprised that someone not close to me had done so much to help my case.

After ten minutes, Mr Symon assured me that the case was based on circumstantial evidence and explained to me what this meant. He assured me that I had nothing to worry about and that I would soon be a free woman. After discussion between the lawyers, but in front of me, they said their goodbyes and left.

I had a troubled night. During the meeting the lawyers had discussed the murder as though I wasn't there. They talked about the large amounts of blood, the dust and the lack of evidence. Yet the reality of it all made my stomach lurch, especially when they discussed the possible but unknown differences between animal and human blood. This played on my mind after they had gone and the ensuing nightmare was one of the worst. In the deeper level dream I was in court where I was found not guilty and acquitted. Feeling relief I woke from the first dream to find myself in the condemned cell prior to being taken to the hanging tower. Just as the rope was put round my neck and I screamed with fear as the trapdoor opened with a thud, I really did wake up, still screaming and sticky with sweat.

The warden who rushed into my cell believed this time it was something more than just a nightmare. She put the lamp to my face and then put it down to take hold of my body. She was trying to calm me and wake me, and she showed sympathy for the first time. Usually it was a rattle on the door yelling, 'For Heaven's sake, Schippan, keep quiet.'

Through my hysteria I tried to tell her what had happened. 'It's the night terrors. Oh it was awful. I felt the hangman's noose around my neck. I can still feel the tightening rope on my skin. I know now what it will feel like.'

The warder agreed, 'Yes, I'm afraid that could happen to you, Schippan, but I hope for your sake it won't come to that. Now try to sleep and not think of such horrible thoughts. There are still some hours to dawn.'

I was too terrified to go back to sleep. Around dawn I was taken from my cell and prepared for the ordeal of the day. I was allowed to dress in my own clothes, which had been beautifully laundered and steam pressed by the women in the gaol. My clothes looked better than I could remember them on the farm, where they were limp and dusty and smelt of old soap. They seemed like new clothes and they lifted my spirits somewhat after the terrors of the night before.

One of the women helped me do my hair and touch up my face. I know that since being confined in prison, my dress that had been loose was somewhat tighter and my once pale and pasty face had gained a bloom. I thought that this had to do with being away from Father and the unexpected pleasant companionship of other women while in a prison. One of the women said, 'We all heard you last night, Mary. It was blood-curdling and even frightened us hard-core women, I can tell you. It sounded as though you were being murdered.'

At nine o'clock Mr Farrell, the keeper from the gaol, led me out to the sallyport where I was placed in the back of a black cab with a woman warden. He sat in the front and we were driven to the Supreme Court. As I arrived in Victoria Square, I could see from behind the thick curtains of the cab, hundreds of people around the front of the building. Minutes before I arrived, the courtroom was opened to the public and there was a mad scramble by the crowds to grab a seat. It was hard to believe people were there just to see what happened to me.

I was ushered through the back entrance and into the court-room where I was told to sit in the dock. As I walked in with my warder I felt all eyes on me and I felt my body flush with acute embarrassment at being put on show like a prize animal. I was thankful for the heavy black veil I was allowed to wear. It helped me in my efforts to distance myself from the events around me, as Mr Symon had instructed me. I was watching someone else's show. When an elderly and sombre judge strode past me in his red robes, we all stood until he took his seat.

Mr Symon took his seat alongside the other lawyers acting on my behalf, Mr Solomon and Mr Foster. I had been told beforehand to watch out for the two crown solicitors, Mr Stuart and Mr Sinclair. They presented a steely and deter-mined union that would have disheartened the most hardened criminal. With thanks for Mr Symon's advice, I willed myself to appear calmer than I really felt and not to feel bullied by them with their knowing looks and cutting remarks.

In his opening address, Mr Symon spoke about how he came to be acting on my behalf. He told the court that Mr Foster had contacted him earlier the day before about the case, and it was only last night, around six thirty, when he was waiting for his train to Manoah, his home in the Adelaide Hills, that he had been handed the brief. He had then followed Foster out of the station to visit me in gaol. Mr Symon said that as my life totally depended on a good defence, it was only fair that the court should be adjourned until at least this afternoon, so he could catch up with all the facts surrounding the case.

There was much muttering and loud sighs of disappointment over this, which prompted a booming, 'Silence in court!' Even Judge Way sighed so heavily that everyone in the court could hear and then he gave Mr Symon a stern look, but responded, 'Till the afternoon is not enough, perhaps it is best that we adjourn until tomorrow morning, same time as now.'

With that he rose, picking up a large book he had been writing in during Mr Symon's opening address, and hurried out in his flowing robes. We followed him. I was driven back to prison and some of the women clapped and cheered when I appeared back so soon, making jokes about the quick verdict. 'That was quick, they must have found you guilty. So tomorrow, Mary Schippan, you'll be hanged by the neck until you are dead.' And they laughed heartily.

The warden instructed me to change my clothes for the prison garb and I was put to work in the laundry with the other women. I was told again, in case I objected, that as a prisoner on remand I wasn't required to work. I told her that as I would be the only prisoner not working and would be left on my own, I would be happy to share their work with them. I was grateful for the noisy but cheerful company.

I thought I was too frightened to sleep that night but due to the lack of it the night before, I slept unusually soundly, free of nightmares. The next morning we followed the same procedure as the day before and when I arrived there were huge crowds again outside the court building and filling Victoria Square. Most of them were women, some armed with lunch bags and babies. The ordeal seemed worse than yesterday, perhaps because I had thought the trial would last only one day, and now there were several police holding back the crowds that heckled and jostled, excited about a woman being put on trial for murder.

The court session began punctually at ten o'clock and I was reminded once more that I had been formally charged with murder. Then I raised my eyes and saw Mother and Father. I had not given them any thought, but seeing my mother obviously suffering jolted my composure. Then there was a procession of witnesses giving evidence.

Practically everyone I knew had come to court to give some account of me. First, my family were called to the stand, followed by Detective Priest. This was followed by friends and neighbours such as little Violet Henke, Mrs Matschoss, Ferdinand Henke, Alby Lambert the district constable, his mother and the journalist from the *Register*, Rodney Cockburn. This went on till the middle of the afternoon. Then Gustave was called to the stand to a hum of expectation, and as the noise grew louder the judge had to call, 'Silence in court!' There was a deadly silence when Gustave was asked if he knew the Schippan family and then how well he knew me.

'I know the Schippan family. I had been keeping company with Mary for about twelve months. I remember being at Schippan's farm on the Sunday before New Year's Day. I came that afternoon and only Mary was home for Mr and Mrs Schippan were away over the hills and Bertha was out playing.'

'How long did you stay?' he was asked.

'I stayed until late evening, until after Bertha had gone to bed.'

'Were you intimate with Miss Schippan?'

'I'm sorry, I don't know what you mean.' Gustave looked around the court as if baffled.

'I'll ask you again. Did anything improper take place between you and Miss Schippan?'

Gustave found this probing question difficult to answer for he took what seemed to be a very long minute before he answered. He glanced at me and I shuddered in acute embarrassment. I'd never known him to lie and he certainly couldn't now that he was on oath. He was to be damned if he lied and damned if he told the truth. Everyone in the courtroom seemed to be holding their breath and no one moved. A hatpin dropping would have been heard while we waited for his reply.

When he answered, 'Yes,' the courtroom erupted into disorder and the judge banged his gavel shouting, 'Silence in court,' as comments from around the courtroom of 'Shame, shame on you' and disapproving 'tut tuts' could be clearly heard. All eyes turned to me before they turned back to Gustave.

His description of the details of our courting activities, such as what we did in the barn and on the sofa in the kitchen in the dark, jolted me. All the time he was answering questions I only once caught him looking at me. He must have known I was staring right back at him from behind the veil, for he nervously played with the hat he held in his hands. After his ordeal he was ushered out of the courtroom.

When the courtroom was finally cleared for the day, my parents had to find their way through the crowds. The warden told me that people were everywhere, hanging on to railings, blocking the path, and climbing on stationary tramcars to catch a glimpse of Mother being supported by Father, or of me, the alleged murderess.

It seemed the crowd of women who were pestering the police were causing a real nuisance by heckling and making loud comments. It surprised me that there were far more women interested in my plight, women who stayed till the bitter end when the court was adjourned at ten o'clock that night. I wondered if they would all be back in the morning. It was difficult for me to know whether they wanted me to be found innocent or whether they were just interested in seeing in the flesh the next woman in South Australia to be hanged.

## 23

Sister Kathleen didn't want me to stop but she had to go. 'Mary, I've chores to do but I'll be back tomorrow. One would never know that all this could happen to one woman. You keep saying I am the first one to hear your story. If I am, I feel privileged.'

The next day Sister Kathleen brought me apples and we moved our chairs out under the verandah and watched the rain, cosy under blankets and shawls as I continued my story.

Gustave was involved in a dramatic incident. Next morning the female warder told me that there were well over 2000 people standing in front of the courthouse, waiting for the day's court session to start. She then told me what had happened to poor Gustave after he left the courtroom just before dusk the day before. He was identified as my sweetheart by someone in the crowd, and they became menacing. At first he was greeted with an ominous stare. Then as he headed down King William Street to stay with relatives of the Schwanefeldts in Carrington Street, he was followed by an angry pack of boys, men and some women who increased their pace as he increased his. Stones and other flying objects began hitting him and he took off his hat and ran for his life, the mob tearing after him yelling, 'Get him. Get him.'

Luckily for Gustave, Detective Priest was outside the court building and saw what was happening. He apparently snatched a bicycle from a nearby constable, telling him he would be back shortly, and pedalled after Gustave blowing his whistle for all he was worth while weaving his way between Gustave's assailants. As he overtook the mob and caught up with Gustave he shouted, 'Quick, for God's sake, son, hop on.' Gustave, white with fear, took no persuading and hopped onto the crossbar of Detective Priest's bicycle. They sped off at great speed leaving the angry and disappointed mob behind screaming for his blood.

Just as the warder was finishing the saga of Gustave's escape and telling me that he was now referred to in the newspapers as my 'pretty lover', the judge strode in and we were called to stand. And we were back to questioning and expert opinions for another day. Witnesses were called one after the other. When Mother was called to the witness stand and asked about our family life and how Father treated us, she lied about his character. When she said, 'He hasn't punished them since they have grown up,' I raged inside as I thought of how we had suffered at his hand and it took all my efforts not to shout out and deny her statements.

When asked about Gustave, Mother said, 'My husband did not object to a well-meaning young man coming to see our daughter.' Of Gustave's behaviour she remarked, 'My husband is a good-tempered man unless anyone fell out with him, then he would get cross.' What an understatement, I thought. When was he not cross? And for Father, 'getting cross' usually meant a physical attack. I was in a rage about how Mother whitewashed Father's character.

The courtroom trial was unlike the more casual inquest two months earlier. It was formal and each point was covered in a great more detail. The men of the law were like mannequins in their wigs and gowns, while the male jury members were unsmiling, severe and a little frightening. Mr Symon worked very hard for me but I couldn't help thinking that most of his pleasure came from taking the stand and being cocky while he twisted everyone's words. Of course, I thought he was wonderful; after all he was my lifesaver. At times I would see the old judge groan or sigh as Mr Symon made some smart remark or other. Then he turned to the judge and spoke of the newspapers: 'I think we should do all that is possible to allay the public curiosity and not whet it.'

Justice Way agreed to this and then reminded the jury, 'Do

not to be influenced by anything you hear outside the court-room but listen to the facts and interpret them carefully. Your verdict will determine the course of a woman's life.'

Following this sobering statement, the witnesses and Dr Ramsay Smith, the state coroner, were requested to be absent from the court during the medical evidence given by the doctor. For some reason Mr Symon did not want the famous Dr Ramsay Smith to stay in the courtroom, and this caused a row. The old judge shouted at him with disgust, 'In my forty years experience, and twenty-six of those on the bench, I cannot ever remember one expert ever being excluded from court during the giving of another's expert evidence.'

But Mr Symon insisted, as calm as a pickled dill cucumber, 'My impression, Your Worship, is that it has been done, although for the moment I cannot put my finger on a specific case, but it was a very high opinion.'

The red-faced judge cut in, 'Can you point to a case? I am inclined to allow Dr Ramsay Smith to remain while Dr Steel relates the facts he saw. When the latter deals with questions of opinion or theories *then* Dr Smith might retire.'

At this insistence by the judge, Mr Symon became quite pas-sionate. He demanded, 'It is impossible for me to do justice to my instructions in the cross-examination of Dr Ramsay Smith if he is allowed to remain while Dr Steel gives evidence as the latter's opinions are mixed up with his statements of facts.' At this point, Mr Symon put Justice Way on the spot when he drew His Honour's attention to Phipson's Law of Evidence.

The judge looked like he was going to explode. He seemed uncertain about the rights and wrongs of Mr Symon's demands, but he wasn't going to be browbeaten by this uppity lawyer. He adjourned the court for ten minutes while he hurried out to consult with a court official, I was told. For a few precious minutes we were allowed to relax a little and the courtroom erupted into noisy chatter which grew into a din. When the judge re-appeared a hush immediately swept over the courtroom and everyone settled once more to concentrate on proceedings.

The judge sat down and staring straight at Mr Symon as if daring him to challenge his decision, bellowed, 'Very well, this is what will happen. Dr Ramsay Smith can stay to listen to the other medical experts unless there is a question of theory or opinion, and then he will have to leave the courtroom. In the meantime I have made the decision that medical experts can hear the evidence of other experts.' As it happened, Dr Smith stayed in the courtroom for the rest of the day.

When Dr Steel gave evidence he caused a stir as he spoke of the problems of the red dust of the Towitta district. Holding a little of it in the palm of his hand, he said it gave a stain that resembled blood, quite a problem with so much stained clothing found at the murder scene. This confusion between traces of red dust and human and animal blood caused much discussion in the courtroom.

Then when giving an account of the stab wounds to Bertha's body he stated, 'In my opinion the cuts were made by a right-handed person from behind.'

The judge cut in, reminding Dr Steel, 'So it is only your opinion that the cuts were made by a right-handed person.' I wondered what the judge knew, what other evidence had he seen to make this statement. Dr Smith took the stand and gave a detailed account of what I was supposed to be wearing at the time of the murder and how many blood spots and smears covered the clothes. He showed no shred of sympathy for my plight, rather he was condemning of me and his account credible to everyone listening. His most damning evidence concerned his observation after digging up Bertha's body twelve days after her burial. 'I extracted fine fair hairs from under Bertha's fingernails that match perfectly those from Mary's head. So was Bertha fighting Mary for her life?'

This statement caused quite a stir in the courtroom. The police and other expert evidence against me looked grim.

I didn't see how I could be found innocent when dozens of specimens of blood-stained clothing, hair, brushes, knives, cloths, rags, knives and bowls were shown to prove the case against me, one after the other.

When all the evidence had been presented I was again asked how I pleaded. I could feel every eye burning into me when, as directed by Mr Symon, I stated in a quiet and girlish voice, 'I am not guilty, sir.' There was an immediate reaction from the court as if they were saying, 'There, I told you so.'

During the summing-up the lawyer for the prosecution, Mr Stuart, proceeded to instruct the jury, 'First, are you satisfied that there was death by violence, and if so does the evidence point to any particular party? As this is circumstantial evidence it is very important, if at all possible, to find a motive and the opportunity when considering the conduct of the person accused.'

To those watching I remained composed and confident, but my body became uncomfortably hot when he said, 'Now, I do not press too strongly on the motive of jealousy. Consider the possibility of another motive. Might the father, an exceedingly good and kind man when his children were behaving properly, treat Mary very severely if Bertha had passed on information she had discovered during the night? I put it to you members of the jury, what would you do in her situation?'

Mr Stuart presented my possible motives, my jealousy over Bertha and my fear of Father, and I was thankful for the veil to hide behind. This man had reached deep into my thoughts and was probing into my soul. Naturally, his convincing plea to the jury alarmed me and in my mind I could see the looming hangman's rope. Just as I pictured myself falling through the trapdoor Mr Symon took the stand and the mood swung in the opposite direction. My dark feelings of impending doom lifted and I could sense instead the heady joy of freedom. He must have known, as surely as I knew, that he held my life in his hands. The point he reiterated, was that there was not sufficient proof of guilt: 'I cannot believe she could have held this ghastly secret in her soul without its getting out somehow. How could she, even if the deed were the outcome of some momentary passion or some temporary and inconceivable madness, have restrained herself from showing some sign? Have any of you detected a sign?'

Not a sound could be heard in the court as Mr Symon pleaded, 'If you, as honest men putting your hands on your hearts can say, without doubt or hesitation, that her guilt seems reasonable, then that is your verdict. But I take the liberty of cautioning you against drawing inferences. A horrible crime has been committed and it has excited our minds. Bloodstained clothes and articles have been produced, all calculated to unsettle our reason and distract our judgement. It would be no wonder, and I should not blame you, if you were disposed to come to a hasty inference on the subject. You will recollect how Macbeth smeared the sleeping grooms with blood and the evidence in this case is exactly similar in character and in degree.' His summing-up seemed utterly convincing; I could not have done the dreadful deed.

I felt confident until it was the judge's turn, but I wanted to swoon when he said, 'The question which you have to consider is whether the deceased died by the hand of the prisoner, or by some other person's. The answer to that question depends on whether you believe the prisoner's statement of what happened on the night. If you do, she is entitled to an acquittal. If you do not believe her and you think she has concocted some mysterious man to take the blame, there is ample evidence in the state of her clothing to justify this conclusion and compel you to find a verdict of guilty.'

I was amazed at how my mood could fluctuate from doom to relief and doom again in the space of minutes. Now my state of mind was such that I wanted to give way altogether and cry in fear, but I kept telling myself, 'Hang on, hang on, Mary. All will be known soon enough.' I was escorted from the courtroom as the jury retired for an agonising two hours to consider their verdict. I was told this was hardly any time at all considering the barbarity of the crime but I, of course, was on a knife edge and every minute seemed an eternity. The warden leaned forward to tell me that there was a crowd of about 3000 people outside also waiting anxiously for the verdict.

It was eight o'clock in the evening and dark outside when the jury informed the court they were ready to give their verdict and we all trooped back into court. The courtroom was lit by gas lighting that roared like a steam train and the heat was oppressive, it seemed worse than it had all day. I could feel the rivulets of sweat running down my face and trickling inside my clothes.

A hush spread over the courtroom as the jury was asked, 'Gentlemen of the jury, are you agreed upon your verdict? How say you? Is the prisoner guilty or not guilty?'

There were a few agonising seconds of silence as a member of the jury rose. The reply was loud and assured, 'Not guilty.' With those two words there was the roar of loud cheers, clapping of hands and stamping of feet in the gallery, and the booming voice of the judge shouted several times above the din, 'Silence in court!'

But the noise did not stop for some minutes. As the news was shouted to those waiting outside, the applause and shouts of excitement rose like an echo from the enormous crowd assembled in Victoria Square and in the streets on either side of the court. A court official shouted, 'Not guilty!' from the balcony of the upper floor.

Sometime later I was told that after Mr Symon's convincing sermon, the verdict of not guilty was expected as was typical when he undertook the defence. I couldn't believe this outpouring of excitement was about me; it was as though everyone was celebrating something entirely different. Then I felt the eyes of the world focused on me at that moment, waiting, waiting, for a response from me. I breathed deeply and set my face to appear as calm as possible while inside my mind was spinning and screaming, 'You're free! You're free!' I looked out through the veil and the mellow glow of the gas lamps made the scene dreamlike. Wave after wave of relief swept over me. So, after all, the jury must have believed my story of the mysterious intruder.

I was far away when I heard a sharp click next to me. I came to my senses to see the bolt to the dock had been shot back and I was being beckoned to step down. My arms were taken by well-meaning people as they guided me from the courtroom to my parents in the courtyard.

It was over as quick as that. No one asked me more questions. There was no more form filling, and no one guiding, holding, or restraining me. The climax of the verdict was over as were the tribulations of the last nine weeks, as quick and as dramatic as that. It was not unlike waking from one of my nightmares and finding nothing remaining of the last few weeks. One moment I was going to be hanged, now here I was surrounded by smiling aunties and uncles, and even my dear brother, Frederick, who had come all the way from the north of South Australia in a rare show of support.

But the worst moment of all was to come. Father was standing in front of me and I felt unease at our coming together once more. The nightmare period of the last few weeks was over, but here I was in another one with Father. It was like one of my nightmares where I woke to find I was still in one – except this time it was for real. The joy of freedom was snuffed out by the reality of being back with Father.

Mother rushed to me and hugged me, saying, 'Thank the Lord, I have one back.' But Father looked at me knowingly, hesitating before he placed his hand on my arm. No word of encouragement but, 'Your uncle's here, Mary, to take us to a hotel for the night.' A small group of official-looking people guided us through to a waiting carriage. Mother, who I know wanted her only remaining daughter home, must have thought very carefully about what it would be like for me to go home with Father. Although I would have to return to Towitta eventually, it had been decided that for now I would be going with my Aunt Giscelia to Eden Valley so I could reclaim something of my shattered life.

The driver of the carriage was one of Mother's brothers. As soon as we clambered aboard he drove off quickly toward the German-owned Black Eagle Hotel in Hindmarsh Square where we were staying the night before heading to Eden Valley in the morning.

## 24

Sister Kathleen, spellbound by my stories, often found it hard to end the meetings when she knew she had to go back to her chores. It had taken many weeks for me to tell her my story because of the little time available. The story would soon be over, but Sister Kathleen was eager to listen to any new snippets I could recall.

'So you were free, Mary, and you eventually went back to Towitta. What was that like?'

Yes I was free. After a few months in Eden Valley I went back to Towitta a free woman, but I knew some of the people in Towitta and Sedan viewed me as a murderess. Although I was found not guilty the case remained unsolved, so I was still viewed as notorious and someone to be feared. No one told me to my face, but things were different for me. In town I'd feel the eyes on me when I climbed down from the wagon. The locals would slink back to let me pass or grab hold of their children's hands as I entered the bakery or post office. Some children even ran screaming when they saw me. Groups of locals whispered to each other as I approached. I heard, 'Mama, is she really the Noon Lady?' as I passed. 'Shhh,' said her mother, with a finger to her lips. The local children called me 'Noon Lady' after the Wendish witch known in folklore for harming infants and children. This hurt me sorely for I was fond of children. In Wendish folklore witches were born with a single tooth and I wondered how many people knew that I had been born with one too. This strange fact would not have helped my reputation. Miserable, I left the town gossip and returned to the farm.

Mother had aged and went about her chores in misery and silence, and brothers Willy and August crept around and whispered to each other. Father, ever tyrannical, put the fear of God into the two boys who leapt to their jobs at speeds never seen before, so afraid were they at what could happen next. Who could they trust now? Although the brothers slept away from the farmhouse in the barn, they were nevertheless anxious about whether the stranger might return to murder them one night. I could never reassure them on this matter; he was, after all, still at large, wasn't he?

Father lost all interest in finishing the new house, and he still had the problem of no spare money. There were only five of us now, and the boys didn't like to come inside the house any more than was necessary. The new house was three feet high, but there it remained, unfinished. A testament to shattered dreams and a family destroyed.

Mother was angry with Father, Father was angry with everyone, and I was angry with Gustave, my sweetheart, who I never saw again.

About nine months after Bertha's death my older brothers Frederick and Heinrich came for Willy and August and took them north to work on a cattle station with them and changed their name so as not to be tainted by the Schippan name. Father kicked up hell when Frederick and Heinrich came for the boys in a horse and wagon because it meant he had no one to labour on his farm and would have to sell up. But they came well armed and there was nothing Father could do to stop them. Needless to say, Mother wailed a lot. I tried to comfort her while I helped the boys gather their possessions and made a hamper of food for them to take on the long journey north. I knew it was their one chance to escape.

A year or so after the boys left we moved from Towitta to Light's Pass, just north of Angaston, and our farm was bought by a neighbouring farmer. The farmhouse soon fell into ruins after the thatch was blown away in a storm. Now there is only the chimney breast remaining; you could pass the site of our farm in the middle of a vast flat wheatfield and never know it was there.

Mother always believed in my innocence, but it was a different matter with Father. We both thought we knew each other's secrets. I remembered all that business with the suspicious deaths of the two hawkers; I knew how dangerous he was.

## 25

Sister Kathleen was most concerned that I had returned to Towitta to live with Father; that I had never made an effort to live elsewhere. 'After all you've been through, I cannot understand why you went back.'

'I did it for Mother. We lived at Towitta for two years after Bertha's murder. It was hard to say whether we chose to become increasingly reclusive, or we were ostracised from the community.'

'It must have been so difficult to share a house with a man like that. I couldn't have endured what you did, Mary.'

Well you have to remember I've had a lifetime of difficult situations, so it was not as hard as you would think. You just learn to withdraw into yourself – and I've always been good at that. But it was lonely and so quiet once there were just the three of us at home. It made for painfully strained evenings. Father read aloud from his Bible and we were his long-suffering audience. I blocked out his voice by concentrating on my tatting or sewing, and daydreaming. Mother and I were expected to pay full attention while he chanted from it or raved on about some grievance or other. Sometimes he made me read a passage and my reading was never good enough. When I stumbled over the pronunciation of words his impatience led him to complain, 'Honestly, girl, I don't know why we sent you to school.'

I'd answer back, telling him, 'It's no surprise, is it? You just remember how often I was needed at home by Mother to help around the farm and look after the brothers and Bertha.' And he'd smack my face for what he saw as an insult to Mother. By now I was past thirty, a spinster, sick and lonely, old enough to have children, yet he still treated me like an impudent child.

Life suddenly changed in 1911, nine years after Bertha died, when Father had a heart attack. When we realised he was dying, Mother sent me to fetch Pastor Stolz. We knew the pastor would be called, Father had told us he had a lot to confess. Confession or not, we guessed he would take dark secrets to the grave. Apart from these secrets how could we forgive him for the brutal treatment he delved out to us throughout our lives?

I sat with Father for an hour before he took his last breath. Earlier that night I had seen the pastor step outside our small cottage at Light's Pass to draw in deep breaths of chill autumn air. Perhaps it was to recover from Father's confession. While the pastor was contemplating Father's last words, I was swooning with sheer joy. Father was dying and his hold on me had vanished forever. It felt like the moment the bolt had been drawn back in the dock when I was found not guilty.

In a small farming community it is easy to believe you know everything about your neighbours, but who knows what goes on behind closed doors? The locals who thought they knew my family must have been divided in their opinions. Some believed that Father was a murderer, while others thought I was. Some thought we both were. Not everyone believed my claim that Bertha was slain by an intruder. Yet I had been found not guilty on the strength of my evidence.

My older brothers told me that the pastor, police and some other local folk believed the answer to the riddle of the murder still lay within our family. With Father's death it was possible that at last everyone would come to know the truth of what happened the night Bertha died. The pastor turned his attention to me. When my oldest brother, Frederick, returned to Adelaide for the trial he told me his friends believed Father had murdered Bertha and I had covered for him. If people believed this I should never have stood trial for murder. I did not care if some believed Father had killed Bertha.

Only Pastor Stolz knew the content of Father's confession. Mother said he'd made his peace with God. The pastor was bound to secrecy and said nothing to me, but following his death shortly after Father's, rumours were rife that the pastor had indeed told someone of Father's confession. When damning rumours about Father's supposed crimes began to circulate throughout the district, we had no idea what was fact and what was fiction.

Father's death freed me but it was all too late. I was melancholy and nervous and in a chronic state of ill health. I grew steadily weaker from the TB that had first been diagnosed nearly twenty years before. And I could hardly bear the agony of losing my sweetheart Gustave. My reputation had been ruined by his courtroom confession of our courtship. It destroyed my relationship with Gustave and any chance of marrying respectably.

After Father died the old pastor often came to see Mother and me. His visits always followed a set pattern. First he would speak with Mother over cake and tea and she would tell him of her woes as she cried. Then having made poor Mother thoroughly miserable he would seek me out, even if I was doing my chores of milking the two cows or feeding the pigs, cleaning the hen house or working in the vegetable garden. He had a severe manner and cold piercing blue eyes. He was fond of preaching that the love of God was more important than the love of one's kith and kin. This was hard to bear for this was what Father had practised – and look what befell our family. All I could think was that there was enough religion to foster hate but never enough to use for love.

The pastor always made sure that what he had to say was away from Mother's ears. I never cared for his attention. It was like he knew more about me than I knew myself. What had Father said in his deathbed confession that suddenly saw the pastor's attention switch to me? In these little sermons – and that's what they were like – he always asked me whether I needed to get any troubles off my chest. He was of the opinion that, like Father, I needed to confess some past dark deed.

'If you tell me what really happened that night, child, the congregation would feel more able to sympathise with you. You probably know some of them are scared of you.'

After his early attempts at trying to draw me out, I screamed at him, 'Look, Pastor, I've told you how it was. What more can I say? I really don't know what you all want from me. As it is now, I'm damned for being innocent. Leave me alone. There's nothing to tell.' After that I ignored his pleas to talk through the ordeal of that night all those years ago. And all the while, the tuberculosis tightened its grip; it interfered with my daily chores. Each day I was a little weaker than the one before. I was dying by inches.

It had been torturous living in Towitta with so many things to remind me of what I had lost: Gustave, my youth and dear Pauline. All four brothers had run away, although you couldn't blame them for that. So we had moved up the hill to Light's Pass. Compared to Towitta, it was hillier, greener and lightly wooded, a much more pleasant place to live. And I walked about the township without feeling an inquisition was constantly taking place behind my back.

Although I no longer felt the centre of gossip, neither was I awash with friends. I mixed with a few women from church, but most women my age were married with broods of children and little time for a single woman with a past like mine. Occasionally I looked after their young children while fending off the straying husbands. The few extra shillings I earned from caring for others' children and the vegetables I sold went into the household kitty.

Though I had a few friends, I no longer had my loving sister to laugh with. I felt the loss of Pauline keenly for she had been my best friend. Our home became as quiet as the grave after Father's death; there was nothing left to fight or talk about.

We moved on but Towitta was not easily forgotten. We were no longer surrounded by vast unprotected windy spaces. In Towitta, our nearest neighbours, who were also our friends, lived half a mile away. At Light's Pass we now had neighbours just yards from the back fence, but few we called friends. The township had its own problems; it was a town divided by affiliation to one of the two Lutheran churches. Families belonging to different congregations were driven apart. Their bitter feuds and squabbles made our situation almost insignificant.

'Sister, I have told you the story of my family and of me. Life with Father was Hell. In the end he destroyed our family and I blame him for the events that befell it. It was only with his death that the remaining but scattered family could feel released from his clutches. By then I was too ill and weary to care and my brothers had left years before. We had to live through years of his cold silence and raging tempers. So now you know a little about our family background, what do you think happened? How do you think Bertha was killed? You must have a theory by now. I started telling you this story in early April and now it is the end of June. Three months of storytelling. And I can tell you I don't feel I have many days left on this earth.'

'Ridiculous, Mary. You're just feeling sorry for yourself. You'll be around for a long time yet.' Puzzled, Sister Kathleen looked at me. 'What a nightmare of a story, Mary. We never believed for one moment that you committed that dreadful crime. We – the non-German folk in the Valley – believed that your father did it. It was so gruesome. A woman wouldn't do it, if you know what I mean. I've always wanted to know how it was that he was never questioned. I believe you've been covering up all along by insisting that an unknown intruder had murdered your sister, to protect your Father and out of fear. Surely you must know this is what we in the Valley all believe?' After a pause she said, 'Well, that's what we were all led to believe.'

I let her ramble on, not quite believing that after seventeen years of silence since Bertha's death I was bold enough to allow these regular meetings to talk about my family, about the murder in my family. What was surprising me was that I now had a strong urge to tell the story and purge my secrets, so I said, 'To tell you the truth, Sister, until the last few weeks I've never heard anyone else's point of view. From the time I was acquitted, no one has dared ask me. We never discussed it at home. Don't forget there was only Father, Mother and me and we hardly spoke to each other. The death of two sisters in a short time was too painful to talk about. There was never anyone who confronted me, so naturally I am interested in what you have to tell me. Only Pastor Stolz wanted to talk about it and I didn't like his manner. Till now, no one but you dared to ask.'

'Oh, Mary, I don't know whether I should be telling you something about what your own poor family has had to endure all these years.'

'Sister, I have no idea what anyone else thinks, that's why I'm asking you for your version. Please tell me, I won't be insulted in any way. I've given you my life story in instalments, but I still don't know what you think or what the general gossip was in the Valley. So now it's your turn to tell me some stories – you can do that on your next visit. It will give you time to think about it.'

# 26

I was keen to hear Sister Kathleen's version of events. When she finally came, we dragged two chairs out under the spreading pepper tree for it was one of those clear sunny winter's days when, if you were well sheltered, the sun could warm. I waited for her to compose herself and begin.

'We agreed that it was my turn to tell you what I know about your family. Please remember I was only a small child then, so this is only what I've been told. The first thing my parents heard from people in Eden Valley was that on the morning following the murder your father's horse was found sweating in the barn. It was said he had ridden the twenty miles to Towitta and back to Eden Valley in the dark. He had intentions to murder the pair of you because you had witnessed him battering one of the hawkers to death years before. And Bertha had asked your father for her own pony or something, and when he wouldn't give her one she threatened to tell the local policeman of his part in the murder.

'The rumour was that Bertha was openly flirting and getting out of control and your father feared she would soon bring shame on the family. He seemed to have some notion that Bertha had been seen with a local youth in a creek bed by a farmer out shooting rabbits.

'I am telling you this, Mary, in the way it was told me, all right? I don't know what's true or what's not.'

I sat there unbelieving, for folk knew more about our family than I knew. It was a good story to hear so long after the event, but it sounded as though she was talking about strangers and not our family at all. I encouraged Sister Kathleen to continue. I was curious to know what else was lingering in people's memory.

'What we heard was that your father rode back from Eden

Valley to your farm that night to do you both in, except you struggled free and managed to raise the alarm.'

'And that's what everyone believes, Sister?'

'Oh, Mary, yes, didn't you know? And then for all these years, out of fear for your own life, you have protected your brutal father. Why you never revealed this ghastly secret, I really can't understand. After all, if you had spoken out he would have been convicted and most likely hanged.'

'I don't mind if that's what people believe, Sister. After all, Father ruled us with an iron fist. But I think you should know, Sister, that it is not possible for anyone to ride over those hills and back to Eden Valley through the night. And further, if Father had done it, I for one would never have protected him. I would gladly have let him hang.'

'Really, Mary? Then what are you saying? If it wasn't your father, are you saying that it was the intruder after all, as you have always insisted?'

'Not at all. There was no intruder other than the ones in my nightmares. I'll tell you the real story for I really do need to get this matter off my chest once and for all. I feel I have so little time left.'

Sister Kathleen didn't answer but looked to me to tell her what really happened. But I was now too tired to continue.

'I am near the end of my story, Sister, but the next part is long and needs to be told in one sitting, if you know what I mean. Perhaps the next time you come, you might be able to stop for longer than usual. I promise it will be the last instalment. It has to be, Sister, for I can feel my days are few.'

'I will come in three days' time then. I am on an early shift that ends about lunchtime. I don't have to dash home but could spend some of the afternoon with you to finish this.'

## 27

*3 July 1919*

It was early afternoon three days later, as she had promised, when Sister Kathleen returned with a basket full of tasty things to eat and drink. 'It's sunny but cold,' she said, 'so let's go and make ourselves comfortable on the enclosed verandah.' She helped me along the corridor toward the long verandah enclosed at one end and settled me comfortably among rugs and cushions brought from my bedroom.

'Are you ready for this, Mary? You really don't have to continue, you know, as I know the story now.'

'I don't think you do, Sister,' I said, and she looked at me puzzled. And so began the last part of my story.

I was a daydreamer. But at night I had nightmares, or as I called them, night terrors, that were so frightening I dreaded going to bed. After Bertha was killed my nightmares became worse. But Father's death brought release, the nightmares ceased altogether. It brought peace but also new problems for me. After his death I was able to think more clearly about what had happened the night Bertha died because I didn't have the nightmares to upset my thoughts. The nightmares I had endured were so horrific that they interfered with what I thought was true and what was not. I know you can't imagine how life can be so warped by nightmares if you've never had them, but it was only when they ceased that I could sort out what actually happened to me on that night all those years ago. And the more I was able to think of the events on that night, the more shocked I became. I felt the need to talk about it but there was no one I could share my fears with. Then I met you, Sister. So long after the event I don't think many other people would care about what I have to say.

In the weeks leading up to Bertha's death our family was not managing at all well. Mother and Father had been invited by Mother's family in Eden Valley to spend some days with them immediately after Christmas. They weren't keen to go as they had so little in the way of gifts and food to take with them, but Mother's brother had insisted. To lessen the number of extra mouths turning up to be fed Father had insisted that he and Mother would go on their own. The four of us, Willy, August, Bertha and me, would stay behind to run the farm. It was a way of saving face with the rest of the family.

As you can imagine we were bitterly upset about this turn of events. We knew our aunt, uncle and cousins were always happy to see us all. And of course we were looking forward to seeing them. We knew that had we gone we would just share whatever we had, because that's what we had done in the past. We had always managed to make a few provisions stretch a long way, a bit like the sharing of the loaves and fishes, which made us feel hearty and full of goodwill. But it was not to be that year, for we were so poor. It was the first time we missed this much-anticipated family event. But for Father's pride, Bertha would still be alive.

Families generally only came together at Christmas. Now there was nothing to look forward to. Even the prospect of seeing Gustave did not fill me with excitement since he had started making excuses about us not going to Adelaide. To add to the general situation I was feeling unwell over Christmas. It was exceptionally hot with temperatures well over a hundred degrees. The heat, disappointment at not spending Christmas with Mother's family, my consumption and the uncertainty of Gustave's affections for me all contributed to my lethargy and misery.

There was the added disappointment of not being allowed to

attend the annual New Year's Eve dance at the Sedan Institute as Mother and Father could not provide a chaperone. Gustave, who may have been considered, was in Adelaide. The stinging attacks on me by both brothers and Bertha because I would not defy our parents' orders did not help my mood. To be twenty-four and left in charge of the farm, yet not be allowed to take them to the dance, was the last straw. I could see bad feeling in the days ahead.

Bertha made a real scene in the afternoon before the dance and throughout the following day. She would not let it rest. Perhaps she had told a young man that she'd meet him there. She was making threats and making a nuisance of herself and by the time she went to bed that evening, I was at the end of my tether.

Before Mother and Father left we ate a miserable Christmas lunch of scraggy roast mutton and a soggy steam pudding. Father made it clear that this year we could not afford to make the usual festival cakes and biscuits and other Christmas trimmings, and we didn't bother with a Christmas tree. There were no treats on Christmas Day and Willy, August and Bertha were bitterly disappointed. After all they were only children.

The boys had helped me catch and slay two sheep for the festivities, mean, skinny animals. When we caught them the boys pretended to have difficulty holding the animals down, so the animals struggled and got free several times before I was able to hold them still enough to slit their throats. I did it in rage and the blood sprayed the clothes I intended wearing for the few days over Christmas. I made no effort to spruce myself up for the occasion as I was past caring.

As soon as Mother and Father departed the boys disappeared with their guns and Bertha hung around like a blowfly and pestered me. 'Mary, why can't we go to the dance? Everyone we know will be there. It's not fair. Mother and Father will never know and we'll behave ourselves.'

'I keep telling you, Father says we can't go and that's the end of it. Stop your silliness. Someone will tell on us if we go, you can be certain of that. Besides, it is not proper for us to come back in the dark without a chaperone. What would people think? You know how they talk about the most trivial of things.'

'But, Gustave could take us. What's wrong with that?'

'You know that can't be. He'll be in Adelaide then and anyway I can't be seen to be going home with him unless we are officially engaged. People would talk about it being improper.'

She smirked, 'Well it is really, isn't it?'

'Whatever do you mean, young miss?'

'It's what you and he do in the barn, or even in Towitta Creek. I've seen you.'

I was outraged, 'Now look here, he and I are going to get married one day and we're sort of engaged.'

'So when you're engaged you can do all that kissing and cuddling and those things that parents do? What would Mother and Father think if I told them?'

'You just dare, Bertha. When you're grown up, you'll know this is what engaged couples like to do. Now be off with yourself. Go and play with the Henke girls for a while. I know Ella and Violet are expecting you to go and see them today. Go and see what Christmas was like for them. They may even give you a present.'

'You only want me to go because Gustave's coming this afternoon, like he did yesterday.'

'So what? I don't want you about while he's here, we have important things to discuss. Just go away and leave me in peace.'

Bertha wore me out with her banter and my mood was not improved when Gustave arrived that Sunday afternoon. He followed me around while I did jobs around the farm. He pleaded with me to stop working and pay more attention to him. I declared I would not stop until the chores were done or until he had given me a date for our betrothal. He was still there in the evening when Bertha was around to hear what was said. The more I pleaded with him to name a date, the more he made excuses as to why he wouldn't do so until he returned from Adelaide in the following week. I rejected his amorous advances but he wouldn't be deterred and before I knew it, I lost myself to his sweet caresses. And he promised to name our betrothal date when he returned from Adelaide. Then he was gone and I was left with my siblings in utter misery.

New Year's Eve came and went and the sour moods continued into the next day, the first day of the new year. That night Bertha went to bed in a huff and hid under the bedclothes. Half an hour after Bertha flounced off to bed, I was just about to go when Willy and August came home. I waited until they had eaten their tea and cake and let them take the only working lamp to their room in the barn. I still felt under the weather and was exhausted from the strain of being in charge and I longed for an early night. Unusually there wasn't even a breeze that night and the silence and pre-moon blackness were eerie. The candles had burned down to stumps, we had planned to make a stack of new ones when Mother and Father returned. In the meantime we had to make do with just the one lamp the brothers took with them.

After the boys left with the lamp, I tried to make amends to Bertha by announcing that it was time for a fairytale in the pitch dark. It could be a cautionary tale, the story of what could happen to those who don't behave. The message to Bertha concerned the trouble that would come her way if she continued to flirt with the boys, especially my sweetheart Gustave. It was also a way for me to let off steam about Father. The stories of Sneewittchen (Snow White) and Aschenputtel (Cinderella) were oft-told ones but I could make them more frightening than most people. That night, impatient and irritated with Bertha, I frightened her with 'How children play butcher', which we often acted out.

The tale was about two children playing together. One pretended to be the butcher and the other one the pig. In the story, the brother playing the butcher was so carried away that he picked up his father's knife lying near the woodpile and grabbed hold of his younger brother. Pulling his head back by his hair, he slit his throat from ear to ear. His mother looked out the window at that moment and saw the little brother twitching and bleeding as he lay dying.

Horrified at what she saw, she ran from the house leaving her toddler daughter in a tin bath. Taking the knife from her son she stabbed him, leaving the two dead sons as she returned to the house to find her little girl had drowned. Full of remorse that her three young children were dead, she grabbed a rope from the woodshed and hanged herself. When her husband came home from hunting and found his entire family gone, he was so distraught that he shot himself dead.

We always worked ourselves to fever pitch as we acted out this grim story and that is how we were on the night I terrified Bertha with the knife, intending to act out the butcher's role. At first she was keen for, like the rest of us, she enjoyed a creepy bedtime story, but then in the total darkness and in my sour and miserable state I became carried away, and she fled back to her bed startled. When I realised what was happening I went outside to recover. I was frightened that what little sisterly affection I may have felt for Bertha had vanished and that I actually wanted to kill her. I sat outside to calm my breathing, listening to the crickets and waiting for the murderous mood to pass. It took some time but then, thinking I had recovered, I went back inside to prepare myself for bed. I had removed my skirt and blouse and climbed into bed and was almost asleep when Bertha blurted out, 'I've got a secret, Mary. A secret concerning your sweetheart, Gustave.'

She had been as cross with me over the Christmas period as I was with her and probably now, more so, because I'd frightened her. I had grown weary of her insolence of the last two days and

I realised now that I hadn't recovered at all from my murderous mood. I shouted into her face, 'What are you saying?'

'Well, you won't sit on the sofa and spoon with Gustave anymore. I heard from Mrs Matschoss today that you no longer have a sweetheart. So, you'll just have to make do with me now.'

'What are you talking about, what have you heard?'

'I can't tell you more, it's supposed to be a secret and I'll get into trouble if I tell you. Anyway, I don't want to say more. You've scared me so much that I never want to hear your horrid butcher stories again. And that's what you are, a butcher!'

I couldn't see her but I leaned over the bed and grabbed hard at her hair and said, 'You'd better tell me what you've heard about Gustave, Bertha, or I will truly hurt you.'

'No,' she protested, 'I won't. You're scaring me.' I pulled harder.

'All right,' she screamed, 'let go and I'll tell you.' She took a breath, 'Mrs Matschoss told me this afternoon that Gustave has had a fiancée for months, but they aren't telling anyone until she turns eighteen at her next birthday. When they've told her father, they'll get married later this year. So you see, he can't marry you too, can he? He can't really be your sweetheart if he's already promised to marry someone else. And you'll never guess who it is?'

My mind was in a whirl. I couldn't imagine how Gustave could have found time to court another sweetheart as he was always travelling to and from Adelaide. I needed to know more. I grabbed her by the hair again and shouted, 'Right, you little hussy, just tell me or I'll really be the butcher.'

'All right, all right, I'll tell, but please, let go, you're hurting me.' She hesitated before adding, 'It's one of his boss's daughters, the prettiest one called Clare. She's the youngest.'

Before I had time to say anything, she continued in a sneering manner, 'And I know what Gustave's been doing here the last few nights – and at weekends too. I know what you've been doing but I bet Father doesn't. He'll be so angry when he finds out what's been going on under his roof.'

'What do you intend telling him? What are you talking about? You're just saying this because you're still angry I wouldn't let you go to the dance or to Adelaide with Gustave. You really can't think that I'd let a young slip of a girl like yourself go all the way to Adelaide with someone like Gustave. It's not done, Bertha. Everyone would talk.'

But Bertha, feeling she had the upper hand, said, 'You know that's not the only reason. You're just jealous about the times he's taken me to Sedan in the past and you couldn't come too. When he asked me to go to Adelaide, even if he didn't mean it, you couldn't bear that either. When he said I was pretty, I let him kiss me right on the lips.'

At this last remark I leaned across once more and grabbed for her hair in the dark and slapped her face hard. 'You are lying, Bertha. Gustave would never say such a thing to a girl so young.' I'd never hit her like that before but she responded by laughing, and then screamed back at me, 'You old witch, well it won't make any difference what you do now, because he can't marry you. And you're only worried that you'll be left holding the baby. I know that's what you're arguing about. Perhaps you'd better marry the local hawker quick because he's about your age,' she screamed. 'You're old, Mary Schippan, old!'

What little control I ever had snapped at this point and another me, from deep inside, took over. My face burned and the blood rushed to my head. Before I knew it I'd rushed to the kitchen and grabbed the largest butchering knife shouting, 'I'll get you, my girl!'

Bertha's laughing became hysterical and she climbed out of bed and taunted me, 'Come on then, get me if you can, Mr Butcher, just like in the fairytale. You know you want to do it. You've been acting for months like you wanted to do it for real.' And I heard her run after me into the kitchen while making the noises of a squealing pig about to be slaughtered. And she was shouting at me, 'You'll have to stay in Towitta for ever now with Father because you're too old to find anyone else to marry.'

The rising moon suddenly appeared briefly from behind the clouds and before it disappeared again I caught a glimpse of her outline in the dark as she passed a window. I saw her eyes flash like a pig's, I heard the squeal, and I snapped. Like the child in the tale acting the butcher, I knocked her forward and heard her fall. And like the butcher with a difficult pig to slaughter, I plunged the long-bladed knife deep into the back of her neck before she had time to recover. She turned and leapt at me and hung on me like a limpet, her nails managing to savagely claw at my hair and my arms. Sticky with her blood, I tried to unclasp her as she began screaming for Willy and August.

Her dullard brothers, whom I had known to sleep through gales and thunderstorms, would never hear her screams from their barn beds a hundred feet away. My head throbbed as Bertha pulled at my hair, kicking and screaming. She was far stronger than me as she fought for her life while screaming, 'He won't marry you now. You'll just become an old witch, Mary Schippan.' I was blind with rage and all the time she laughed, taunting me still and following me into our parents' bedroom.

Then suddenly the laughing stopped and I heard her slump to the floor in the pitch darkness. She laughed just once more, but stopped as though gagged and then there was silence. I felt about to find her stretched out on the floor on her stomach. I pulled her head up by her hair and, putting the knife into my cutting hand, I slashed her from ear to ear with my best pig and sheep-cutting strokes, I don't know how many times.

Sister Kathleen was silent when I paused. 'Are you all right, shall I go on?' Although she looked stunned and her voice wavered, she answered, 'Yes, don't stop now.'

I say it all happened like this for I can only think that's what must have happened. Or perhaps it was a nightmare and someone else did it. I don't know. What I knew was Bertha lying there, in the bedroom, unmoving. Surely not my little sister.

The night was still except for chirping crickets. I sat down for a few minutes and collected my thoughts. I stung from the scratches on my legs and arms and where the blade of the knife had nicked my shoulder. My head ached from where hair must have been pulled out by Bertha. And it was as I was sitting there that I realised what I had just done. I had just killed my sister like she was a pig over a silly squabble. I was terrified at what I had done. I will be hanged, I thought. Yet, I wasn't really sure that I had done anything. What happens now, what will I do? I had to invent something plausible for the brothers, but what? Think, Mary, think.

I calmed my nerves and as I did so I could see that it was now lighter outside than in. I could now see Bertha lying on her stomach with her arms outstretched. As if mocking me, the soft and silvery moon that had been hiding behind one of the barns rose above it and began streaming through the window onto the bloody scene. It shone on the knife on the floor in the kitchen. I stepped in warm sticky blood as I picked it up and walked around in my damp stockinged feet clutching the knife trying to find a place to hide it. I went through the front door, and stretching up toward the thatch roof I drove the knife deep under the thatch. At the pump I took off my stockings and other underclothes to rinse them. I washed my face and hands sticky with blood and plunged my head under the pump to rinse my hair. The night air was stifling and it would dry in minutes. I then redressed in my wet clothes and walked around the yard under the moonlight until they had dried.

All this time the old dog that was tethered by a chain some yards from the house had not stirred from his sleep. Nor had any sound come from the barn where the boys slept. I realised I had to convince my brothers that a stranger had come into the house. Yes that would do. I'd invent an unknown intruder, like the goblin in my nightmares. I dressed in my blouse and old skirt and I ran around the yard, working myself into a hysteria that, after what I had just been through, wasn't difficult. I then ran to the barn where I shouted for August and Willy. They didn't stir and so I shook them. 'What's the matter, Mary?'

'Quick. One of you will have to go to Henkes'. There's a strange man in the house, he's got a knife and Bertha's in there and I don't know what's happening. Oh hurry up, August. I'll stay here with Willy until you return.'

Willy was terrified at the thought of a dangerous man on the loose and began crying. I told him to keep quiet until August returned and that we had to sit in the dark in case the stranger came looking for us. I deliberately stirred up his fear.

August returned without Mr Ferdy Henke, who had refused to come, believing we were concocting a story. So armed with rakes and stakes and a gun we marched over to the house. On reaching the back door we lost our nerve and instead set off to Alf Lambert's house. The local constable lived almost a mile away. By this time Willy was almost hysterical with fright but I tried to comfort him in the best way I could.

It seemed to be hours before we came back with the constable. He lit the lamp and we all followed him into the house with sticks and forks. I held onto Willy's hand while the constable, followed by August, cautiously crept through the kitchen to the bedroom. The lamp shone on the body of Bertha stretched out across the floor. The brothers gasped in horror at what they saw and the constable yelled, 'Out of here, quick. There's been a murder and I must get help.'

As we retreated I grabbed my boots from under the sofa and put them on over my burr-covered stockings. We blew out the lamp and ran back across the silvery fields now bathed in moonlight towards Constable Lambert's house. It was about midnight when Mrs Lambert, his mother, made us each a makeshift bed in which to sleep while her son saddled his horse and rode to Truro for reinforcements.

It was almost dawn and already hot when I awoke. I was alarmed to find myself in a strange bed and it took some time to remember where I was and how and why I came to be there. I felt confused, were the events of the night before a nightmare? And I ached from head to toe, I was covered in scratches and my head throbbed.

Mrs Lambert provided me with a large bowl of cool water in the outhouse and I did my best to wash and tidy myself before finishing donning my dusty and shabby clothes. We sat around shocked and silent until Constable Lambert returned and we then followed him and his mother back across the paddocks to our farm. He never once asked me questions about what had happened, so I remained silent. When we arrived back, they stripped Mother's bed and spread it with an old blanket. Bertha was laid there on her back and washed down, but there was no attempt to clear up the blood on the floors or walls.

Shortly after, the place was abuzz with police and locals trying to find out what was going on. I sat on the bench outside the farmhouse. The boys told me they were going to look around the farm for clues. That night I slept in the barn with the brothers and next morning Detective Priest, the very one I had met a couple of years earlier, arrived with a large group of reinforcements.

News certainly travelled fast by the bush telegraph for Mother and Father returned from Eden Valley the next day. The boys attended to the horse while Mother wrapped her arms around me and asked what was going on. She told me that she had heard some news in Eden Valley the night before and they had made tracks for home at first light.

## 28

Following this confession to Sister Kathleen, I began to cough. I held the cloth to my mouth to catch the blood. It was some minutes before I could stop. Sister Kathleen rushed to my side and after my coughing bout had passed she said, 'This is such a horrible time for you. I wish it didn't have to be like this.' After cleaning me up, she said, 'Now look what you've done to yourself. This kind of excitement is not good for your condition, it could bring on a fit. You know there's no need to make up such a story just because you feel guilty about what happened so long ago.'

Although weakened by the retching, I still protested, 'But, Sister, I am not making this up. Don't you realise that what I am telling you now is true? Why I am not mad with the guilt, I don't know. Had Father lived longer, I would be in the lunatic asylum where that Schwanefeldt girl was sent.'

'Who is she?' interrupted Sister Kathleen.

'She's the girl my sweetheart Gustave was supposed to be engaged to, whom I knew nothing of until that dreadful night. After all that fuss and bother following the confession at the trial, Mother told me that Mr Schwanefeldt had sacked Gustave. They had not known that all the time he was planning to marry their daughter he was also making overtures to me. After the admissions in court of his affair with me, the girl's parents didn't think he was a suitable person for their daughter to marry. They sacked him and warned him to stay away from her. She, poor girl, had a nervous breakdown and was eventually incarcerated in the Glenside lunatic asylum. As far as I know she's still there after all these years ranting and raving about cutting throats.

'Gustave also had a hard time at the hands of his own family. He ended up with no job and no sweethearts and was beaten by his older brothers. A passage was booked for him from Port Adelaide to Queensland. His brothers forcibly put him on the ship and sent him to stay with relatives so he could work in the cane fields far north of Brisbane. He later changed his name, married someone else and had a family.'

'I had no idea.'

When I told Sister Kathleen that I was beginning to feel cold even though we were sitting in warm sunshine, she put a blanket around my shoulders and over my knees and propped up my pillow. She had been so kind to me since I was brought into the Consumptive Home a few months before when the disease had returned with a vengeance. My life was fast slipping away from me and I was confined to days of sitting about or long sleeps. Before I became too ill Sister Kathleen had promised to take me to Semaphore to look at the sea. But I knew now I would never see it.

She straightened my pillow and looked straight into my eyes and said seriously, 'But how can this story be true? I remember that case so well for I read about it in the old papers that my parents had kept. They never threw them out, you know, because the murder was so sensational. And of course everyone spoke about it for ages at family gatherings and at mealtimes. We all know you couldn't possibly have done it because you are left-handed and the newspapers wrote that the murderer was right-handed.'

'Well that may be so, Sister. But you see, what no one bothered to find out was that I can use both my hands equally well. There's a special name for it, I'm told. Further, when I helped my brothers with the slaughtering of a pig or a sheep, I would hold the pig down with my left hand while slitting its throat with my right hand. I always did it that way.'

'Mary, you really do know how to tell a good story, but you know you shouldn't tell tales quite so realistically for one day someone might believe you. If I didn't know you better, I would have believed that story. And that stuff about Bertha thinking you were expecting a baby. If that was true, what was that about? I don't remember hearing anything about a baby in this story before.'

'Only Gustave and the women in the Adelaide Gaol knew I was expecting. The women were helpful. One of them, Melissa, was very helpful. When we got together for our sewing afternoons, we would tell each other of our supposed crimes. She told us that she had got caught after one of her special operations had gone wrong. One afternoon she whispered to me, "Tell me, dearie, you're in the family way aren't you?"'

'Well, I broke down there and then partly from the relief of having a shoulder to cry on. My clothes were tightening around my waist and I'd already let out the seams once. It was only going to be a matter of time before this news leaked out.

'"Look, I can help you," she told me. "I know what a desperate state you are in and I'm quite experienced in situations like this. Your trial's coming up soon and believe me, you'll have even less hope of escaping that noose once everyone knows your true condition. Even if you get off, you'll still be having a baby out of wedlock and you'll be just as damned. Further, if we don't do this little operation soon, it will be too late for you to have one at all. I can do them easily and quickly but not if you're more than three months gone. Would you like me to help you?"'

'"Please."'

'"It's quite easy, we'll do it tomorrow afternoon. As you know when we're all together in the sewing room we're watched by the warden like a hawk. However, there is about ten minutes when she takes the repaired overalls from us and takes them back to stores. She must trust us but I don't know how she gets away with it. In those few moments we are unsupervised I'll be able to help you."'

'So the next day when the warden walked away with the load of repairs, the women laid me out on the table and Melissa swiftly performed her operation with a knitting needle, the same one used by the women who knitted clothes for babies and children so Mrs Maughan, the clergyman's wife, could give to the poor in the West End of Adelaide. You can see there were no secrets there.

'Melissa told me to expect the results of her handiwork about the next day or so. And so it happened. We were in the sewing room two days later when I started to feel things start. I asked to use the privy and everything happened without a fuss. It was a rough few nights for me; that's when I had some of my worst nightmares about being hanged. I had a fever for a few days but then it passed. Following the miscarriage I felt a bit down for a few days but the women kept my spirits up and protected me from any possible exposure.

'About a week later when we were at our sewing one afternoon, a lawyer came into our sewing room with one of the wardens. The warden shouted out, "Madam Harpur, sorry, I mean Missus Melissa Fairbairn, you have a visitor." At that moment my blood ran cold. I realised my operation had been performed by none other than the woman who had killed Rebekah.'

Sister Kathleen didn't bat an eyelid and I don't think she really understood the full impact of what I had been telling her for she said, 'Look, I'd better get back to the ward. I'll help you back to your room because the sun is going down and it is cooling down quickly.'

So Sister Kathleen assisted me back to my room and saw me into my bed before she said, 'Mary, that was one of your best stories, seemingly so believable.'

'But, Sister, it *was* a true story, you must believe me.'

But she laughed in response and as she left the room she repeated, 'Yes, that was a good story, Mary.'

And I was left alone with my first and only confession.